Stephanie Olds

A BREATH
OF RAIN

A Breath Of Rain by Stephanie Olds

Copyright © 2025 by Ink and Revival Publishing

Printed in the United States of America
First Edition—Second Printing, May 2025
ISBN: 978-1968178031

Ink and Revival Publishing
Virginia, USA

"To everyone who has ever been told their disability defines them—you are more than your limitations.

To those who have fought to be understood, to be seen, to be believed—your struggle does not diminish your strength.

And to every single person who has learned to embrace who they are, despite the world's expectations, I celebrate you.

You are not broken. You are not less.

You are resilient. You are extraordinary.

Keep standing tall. Keep moving forward.

You are unstoppable."

TABLE OF CONTENTS

CHAPTER ONE

ANHIDROSIS

I always knew I was different. I just didn't know why.

Growing up in South Louisiana, heat was a part of life.
The air was thick with humidity, the kind that clung to your
skin and wrapped around you like a heavy blanket. It
wasn't just hot—it was the kind of heat that made you feel
like you were breathing through a wet towel, like the very
air around you was pressing down, making every
movement slow and heavy.

By mid-morning, the world shimmered under the sun,
waves of heat rising from the pavement, making the road
ahead look like it was melting. Even the trees seemed to
struggle under the weight of it, their branches hanging low,
their leaves still, as if too exhausted to rustle. The cicadas
never stopped their high-pitched droning, a constant hum in
the background, like a reminder that the sun wasn't letting
up anytime soon.

In the afternoons, you could see how the heat shaped

everything around us. The stray dogs that normally trotted up and down the street disappeared into the shade, their tongues lolling from the effort of simply existing. The neighborhood cats weren't much better, sprawled on porches, moving only to stretch or shift into a slightly cooler patch of shade. Even the birds seemed quieter, too tired to sing, perching in the thickest parts of the trees where the air might be just a little cooler.

People had their own ways of dealing with the heat. Mr. Reggie, our next-door neighbor, was out every morning at dawn, mowing his yard before the sun got too high. He always wore the same thing—faded denim overalls, a white tank top, and a straw hat that had seen better days. By the time the sun really started bearing down, he was done. He'd settle into the old metal chair on his porch, a red bandana hanging from his neck, and drink sweet tea from a sweating glass. He'd sit there for hours, watching the street, waving at folks passing by but never moving too much—because moving meant sweating, and sweating meant more effort to stay cool.

The rest of us did whatever we could to survive the day. Kids rode their bikes in slow, lazy circles under the shade of the oak trees, careful to stick to the patches of pavement that weren't scorching hot. The blacktop on the streets got so hot that if you pressed your hand to it for more than a second, it felt like it might burn clean through your skin. Nobody needed to be told not to go barefoot—we learned that lesson quick.

Mothers carried paper fans in their purses, fanning themselves absentmindedly as they stood outside chatting with neighbors, the occasional "*mmhmm*" or "*you don't say*" punctuating their conversations. Their voices were slow, drawn out by the heat, as if speaking too fast would take too much energy. Every few minutes, one of them would press a cold bottle of soda or iced tea to their neck, sighing as the coolness cut through the thick air for just a moment.

The old folks sat on their porches, watching the world move around them, drinking ice water or homemade lemonade, the condensation from their glasses dripping onto the wooden railings. They rocked back and forth in their chairs, the rhythm steady, like the creak of the wood was part of the day's natural soundtrack. They'd call out to passing kids with warnings disguised as wisdom.

"*Y'all don't run too hard now, you'll drop dead in this heat.*"

"*Take a break in the shade before you burn up.*"

"*You better not be out here actin' a fool and end up with heatstroke. I ain't gon' be the one draggin' you to your mama.*"

The rule was simple: once you went outside, you stayed outside. No running in and out of the house. Every grandmother, every mother, every household had the same rule.

"*Don't be runnin' in and outta my house, lettin' all the cool air out. I don't have enough money to air condition the entire neighborhood!*"

3

It didn't matter where you were or whose house you were near. That rule was universal. The adults weren't trying to hear kids begging to come inside and cool off. You were supposed to *"play outside"*, not loiter in the kitchen, letting cold air hit your back while you *"decided"* if you were thirsty.

And that's why drinking from the garden hose wasn't just normal—it was necessary. Nobody questioned it. If you got thirsty, you found the nearest house with a hose, turned the spigot on full blast, and let the water gush out. The first few seconds were always scalding hot, like it had been stewing inside the hose all morning, but then it would turn cool—maybe not ice-cold, but cool enough to be refreshing. You'd lean down, mouth open, gulping it straight from the stream or cupping your hands under the flow. If somebody was feeling generous, they'd let the water trickle down their fingers so the next kid in line could drink without getting sprayed in the face.

Nobody worried about bugs, or germs or whether the hose had been sitting in the sun too long. If you were playing outside, you were sweating (well, everybody but me), and if you were sweating, you needed water. That was just how it was.

Sometimes, if you were lucky, a grown-up would get the idea to turn the sprinkler on in the yard. Kids would rush over, peeling off their shoes and throwing themselves into the freezing spray, screaming and laughing as the cold water soaked their clothes. It didn't matter if you weren't wearing a swimsuit—nobody cared. The heat made you desperate for relief.

Even if no sprinklers were involved, there were always ways to cool down. Somebody's dad might pull out an old metal washtub, fill it with hose water, and let the little kids sit in it like a makeshift kiddie pool. A family might spread out an old plastic tarp covered in dish soap and water creating a homemade slip-and-slide. Or someone's mama would walk outside with a tray of red and orange popsicles, passing them out like they were gold, warning everybody, *"Y'all better not drop these on my porch, I "mean" it."*

But no matter what, the heat never truly went away. It was just something you got used to, something you worked around. People adjusted their movements, slowed their pace, sought shade whenever they could. It was like an unspoken agreement between us and the sun—we knew it wasn't going anywhere, so we found ways to live with it.

For most kids, it was just part of life. For me, it was something I had to survive.

The houses in our neighborhood were built for the heat. Wide porches stretched across the fronts, offering shade that made the difference between unbearable and just barely tolerable. Ceiling fans whirred in every room, stirring the thick air, even though it never really got cool inside. The best place to be was right in front of a box fan, letting the air hit you full force while you pressed an ice-cold bottle of soda to your forehead.

Even still, there was no real escape from it. The heat seeped into everything. It made the inside of the car feel like an oven if you left the windows rolled up, the steering wheel and seats would be too hot to touch. It made clothes stick to your skin, made the air heavy with the scent of sweat, bug spray, and the sharp, sweet smell of hot asphalt. It turned the simplest things—walking to the mailbox, sitting on the porch swing, even just standing outside for too long—into a slow, sweaty battle against the sun.

And yet, somehow, life went on. People worked, played, ran errands, and went about their days like the heat was just another part of the world—because, in the deep south, it was.

But for me, it wasn't just an inconvenience. It was a force I had to fight against, something I could never quite outrun. While my siblings and the other kids ran through sprinklers, laughing as the water cooled their flushed skin, I stayed inside, pressing my palms against the cool tile floor, trying to shake the feeling that I was burning up from the inside out. While others wiped sweat from their brows and kept going, I struggled just to stay upright, my body refusing to do the one thing that might have helped.

The heat was everywhere, and for me, it wasn't just uncomfortable—it was dangerous.

It was a part of life, but it wasn't one I ever got used to. My siblings—five of them, all older—could handle it just fine. They played, running around outside for hours, their brown faces glistening with sweat, their clothes damp by the time they came inside. But for me, being outside was never as fun as it looked. I wanted to climb jungle gyms, race across the park, and chase fireflies until the sun dipped below the horizon—just like they did. But the heat always got to me too fast. Instead of excitement, all I felt was a heavy, suffocating discomfort that made it impossible to enjoy the games. While they played without a second thought, I was always the first to sit down, the first to look for shade, the first to wish for rain. For as long as I can remember, there was one thing about me that never made sense—I didn't sweat. Not even once.

When I was a toddler, they thought I was just picky about the heat. While my brothers and sisters raced barefoot across the yard, I'd stay on the porch, shifting uncomfortably in my little summer dresses. Mom said I used to cry when they tried to make me play outside. But put me in a swimming pool? I could float for hours, the cool water easing the heat that always felt too much for me. On rainy days, I'd rest my forehead against the window, watching the droplets streak down the glass, wishing I could step outside and feel that same relief.

At first, my parents didn't think much of it. *"Lily's just delicate,"* Mom would say, holding a concerned hand to my forehead while my siblings wiped sweat from their brows. *"She don't sweat easy like y'all."*

Hearing that made me feel special. But as I got older, I started to wonder if it was normal. Why did everyone else sweat when they ran, but I didn't? Why did my face stay dry while my friends' shirts clung to their backs?

The first time it really scared me, I was four years old.

It was the Fourth of July, and our neighborhood was having a big barbecue. The smell of ribs and smoked sausage filled the air, music played from somebody's speaker, and the heat—*Lord, the heat*—was thick and unrelenting. Kids ran barefoot through the grass, chasing each other, their faces slick with sweat. I wanted to join them, and for a while, I did.

At four years old, I wasn't thinking about my body's limits. I just wanted to be a part of the fun. The older kids were playing tag, their laughter ringing through the humid air as they darted around picnic tables and weaved between folding chairs. I ran after them, my little legs working as hard as they could to keep up. For a moment, it felt good, being part of the chase. But it didn't take long before my chest started feeling tight, my arms heavy, my skin burning—not from the sun, but from the heat trapped inside me.

I slowed down, pretending I wasn't really trying to win the game anyway. When no one was looking, I wandered over to where a group of kids were tossing water balloons. Their hands were wet, their clothes damp from the splashes, and I wanted nothing more than to feel that cool relief on my own skin. I picked up a balloon, its surface slick and smooth in my hands. I tried to throw it, but my fingers fumbled, and instead of soaring through the air, it dropped right at my feet and burst, sending a splash of cool water up my legs.

For a second, I sighed in relief. The cold water felt so good, but just as quickly as it had come, it was gone, leaving nothing but the heavy heat pressing in again. The other kids kept throwing, laughing as balloons exploded against arms and backs. I wanted to stay, to beg them to throw one at me just so I could feel the cold again, but the game was moving too fast. I was already too tired.

I wandered over to where my mom was sitting with the other ladies, fanning themselves with paper plates and sipping from tall glasses of iced tea. She looked down at me, brushing a stray curl from my face. *"You okay, baby?"* she asked, her voice soft but knowing.

I nodded, not wanting her to make me go inside yet. *"I wanna do sparklers."*

It wasn't dark yet, but some of the adults had already pulled out the long, thin sparklers, lighting them for the kids who waved them through the air in bright, glittering circles. Daddy was over by the grill, his face slick with sweat, but he smiled when he saw me tugging at his shorts. *"You wanna try one, Lil' bit?"*

I nodded again, and he crouched down, holding a lighter to the tip of the sparkler until it burst to life, little golden sparks dancing in the air. He handed it to me carefully, his hands hovering near mine just in case.

I grinned, waving the sparkler slowly, watching the light trace patterns in the thick evening air. This, I could do. It didn't take running or jumping or sweating like the other kids. Just standing still, letting the tiny fireworks dance in my hands.

But even then, the heat clung to me, wrapping around my body, making my head feel fuzzy, my legs wobbly. I didn't say anything, though. I just held onto my sparkler, trying to stretch out the moment as long as I could

Then, it happened.

At first, it was just a feeling—heavy, sluggish, like the sun was pressing down on me harder than everyone else. My skin burned, but not like a sunburn. More like fire ants underneath my skin. The world tilted, my head swam, and suddenly, everything went dark.

When I woke up, I was in the backseat of our car, the AC blasting cold air against my face. Mom was holding my hand tight, and Dad was driving, his knuckles white against the steering wheel.

"You passed out, baby," Mom said, her voice tight with worry.

I didn't understand. I wasn't sick. I wasn't tired. But something was wrong.

That was only the beginning.

———

CHAPTER TWO

ELEMENTARY SCHOOL

I t kept happening—at the grocery store, in the yard picking pecans, even on warm autumn afternoons when the heat wasn't as bad. Every time, my body would feel heavy, my head would spin, everything would start turning white and I'd have to sit down before I collapsed. My parents started watching me more closely, making sure I always had water, making me stay inside when it got too hot.

But at school? It felt like nobody really cared.

It wasn't that my teachers were cruel or that they wanted me to suffer. It was just... I don't think they really *got* it. The idea that a child could just *not* handle the sun, that it wasn't a matter of preference but a real, medical condition, didn't seem to compute. If I had asthma, maybe they would have paid more attention, kept an inhaler on standby, made accommodations to keep me safe. But a kid who *"just didn't do well in the heat"*? That sounded like whining.

Drama. Something I was choosing rather than something my body forced on me.

So every single recess, while the other kids screamed and laughed, playing tag, tether ball, or swinging from the jungle gym, I sat. I found my place on the painted white line along the pavement, book in hand, and *stayed there*. I wasn't much of a rule-breaker, but even if I had been, there wasn't much else I *could* do. Recess was non-negotiable, and so was being outside for it. The only way I could manage was to sit perfectly still, not exert myself, not invite the dizziness that would leave me sprawled on the ground.

The teachers must have thought I was anti-social, the weird little girl who never played, never ran, never joined in. They never asked *why* I sat alone. Never thought to check if I *wanted* to be there or if I was making the best out of a situation I had no control over.

And in their defense, I guess they had never heard of anyone simply *not being able* to do the sun. Heat stroke? Sure, they understood that. But that was something that happened to kids who forgot to drink water, who played too hard, who pushed their limits. Not something that happened just from *being outside.*

So they never made exceptions for me. Never gave me a cool spot inside to sit, never considered letting me wait in the shade by the cafeteria doors. If I was quiet and well-behaved, they let me be. And if they *did* notice me sitting there, always reading, always keeping to myself, they probably thought I was just different.

Maybe even a little difficult.

On the worst days, when the heat was at its most brutal, I'd watch the other kids, their hair clinging to their foreheads, their shirts damp with sweat. They were *miserable*, too, but they could still *play*. The heat was uncomfortable for them, but it wasn't a threat. Their bodies knew how to handle it.

Mine didn't.

I started to resent the way the other kids could bounce back from the heat, the way they could take a break, drink some water, and jump right back into their games. I hated how easy it was for them, how *"normal"* it was to be able to run, sweat, cool down, and keep going. And most of all, I hated how nobody seemed to notice how much I was struggling.

But then, there were rainy days.

Rainy days were my secret joy.

Because when it rained, there was no recess. No forced time outside. No sitting on that stupid painted line, pretending I was perfectly content with my book while my head ached and my skin burned from the trapped heat inside me, cooking me like a rotisserie chicken.

On rainy days, we stayed inside. We watched movies or did quiet activities at our desks. No running, no sweating, no almost fainting. Just *existing* comfortably for once.

I don't think anyone ever noticed how much I "loved" the rain. To them, it was just another day, maybe even a disappointing one since they couldn't go out and play. But to me, it was peace. It was the only time I got to feel normal.

I never told anyone that. Never let on how much I wished for those gray clouds to roll in, for the sky to open up and give me just one day where I didn't have to pretend that I was okay outside.

Because outside, under the burning sun, I never was.

Kindergarten was kicking my butt. But it wasn't just playtime that was a problem. I hated leaving the classroom at all. In my city, walking anywhere outside meant stepping into a wall of heat so thick it could knock the breath out of you. A trip to the cafeteria, the auditorium, or the library was enough to make my vision blur and my knees wobble. I started dreading those moments, knowing that every time I stepped into the sun, I was risking another near-fainting episode.

That's when I came up with a plan.

Whenever I felt that dizziness creeping in, I'd step out of the line and squat down to untie and retie my shoelaces—real slow, like I was making sure they were just right. I'd focus on the ground, taking deep breaths, letting the moment pass. It gave me just enough time to steady myself, to cool off a little before standing back up. And if I did faint, at least I wouldn't fall as hard from down there.

It worked, mostly.

From the very first day of kindergarten, I knew school was going to be a challenge. Not because of the books or the lessons—I loved those. It was everything else. The parts of school that other kids didn't have to think twice about. The heat. The walking. The endless activities that required running and playing outside, things I simply "couldn't" do the way they could.

My kindergarten classroom was plumb on the farthest edge of the school campus, so far out it felt like they stuck us there as an afterthought. A whole football field—or more—stood between us and the cafeteria, a distance that felt even longer in the blazing heat. The first few weeks, I tried my best to keep up with the other kids as we made the daily trek to lunch, but it didn't take long for me to realize how much harder it was for me than everyone else.

By late August, the heat was merciless. The kind of heat that made the pavement shimmer like water, that made the air so thick it felt like you were breathing through a cotton comforter. The other kids complained about it, sure, but they could handle it. They'd huff and puff about how hot it was, but they kept moving, their foreheads damp with sweat, their faces red with exertion. Me? I had no way to release the heat that built up inside me. And every single day, that long walk from the classroom to the cafeteria was like a slow march toward disaster.

Luckily, I had my plan, though.

It was my little trick, my way of giving my body a moment to recover without drawing too much attention to myself. But on this particular day, my plan failed.

It started the way it always did. Halfway to the cafeteria, I felt it creeping in—the heavy feeling in my head, the way my vision blurred just slightly around the edges, the sickening warmth that made my stomach churn. I knew I had to stop. I slowed my steps, letting the line move ahead of me, and bent down, reaching for my laces with fingers that didn't feel quite steady.

Then—everything tilted.

Before I could brace myself, my legs gave out. Instead of simply squatting down like I meant to, I lost all control and toppled sideways, crashing off the sidewalk and into the dry, patchy dirt beside it. The world spun, a jumble of blue sky, brown earth, and tiny pebbles digging into my skin. Everything was a white blob. Then, everything went dark.

When I came to, I was on my back, my face hot, my mouth dry. The sun was still there, glaring down at me, but now there were blurry figures around me—my teacher, some of my classmates, and a couple of older kids from a nearby grade. I could hear my teacher's voice, high and anxious.

*"She just **collapsed!**"*

Someone else muttered, *"She was walking so slow, I thought she was just tired."*

I tried to sit up, but my limbs felt disconnected, too weak to move. My teacher crouched beside me, pressing a hand to my forehead, then frowning when she felt no sweat.

"*She's dry,*" she said, almost to herself. "*It's **too** hot out here for her to be dry.*"

Minutes later, the school nurse arrived with a wheelchair, and they whisked me away to the front office, where they handed me a small cup of water and started asking me questions.

"*Did you eat breakfast this morning, sweetheart?*"

"*Do you feel sick, or just weak?*"

"*Do you get dizzy often?*"

I answered as best as I could, but my voice felt small, lost in the grown-ups' worried murmurs.

Then, my parents arrived.

Mom came in first, her face tight with concern. Dad was right behind her, his hands clenched into fists at his sides like he was trying to hold something back. They both rushed to my side, but before they could even speak, the principal stepped in.

"*We're very concerned,*" she said, her voice carefully measured. "*Lily fainted on the way to lunch. Given the circumstances, we have to consider all possibilities, including malnourishment.*"

Mom's expression went from worried to shocked in a heartbeat. *"Excuse me?"*

The principal sighed like this was something she hated having to do. *"We just need to be sure Lily is getting proper nutrition at home. She collapsed before even reaching the cafeteria, and we've noticed she doesn't seem to have the energy of the other students."*

My father's voice was sharp. *"Because she **can't** handle heat like other kids. We've been trying to get doctors to take it seriously for years!"*

But it was clear they had already made up their minds. They saw a little girl fainting before lunch, a little girl who never quite kept up with the other kids, and they thought the worst.

A few days later, Child Protective Services knocked on our door.

The CPS visit was one of the most confusing moments of my young life. I didn't understand why strangers were in our house, asking my parents questions, checking our kitchen cabinets, peeking into my bedroom like they were looking for something out of place.

One of the ladies knelt down to my level, her smile too tight.

She was an older white woman, heavyset with a stiff

posture that made it seem like she didn't want to be here—but also like she wanted to *find* something. Her hair was over processed, a brittle shade of yellow that clashed against her too-dark eyebrows. Thick layers of foundation sat on her skin like paint, her bright pink lipstick bleeding into the tiny lines around her mouth. She smelled strong—too much perfume, the kind that made my nose wrinkle.

She wasn't dressed like someone who visited kids' homes for a living. Her blouse was silky and hot pink, stretched tight over her stomach, and her long acrylic nails clicked against the clipboard she clutched like it held my family's fate. Her eyes, lined with heavy black pencil, flickered over me with something close to disapproval.

The other woman stood a few feet behind her, watching.

She was much younger, maybe in her late twenties, with deep brown skin and a head full of thick curls. She was tall and slim, wearing a simple gray pantsuit that looked comfortable but professional. Unlike her partner, she didn't seem eager to catch my parents in a lie. Her expression was softer, her warm brown eyes scanning the room with curiosity rather than suspicion.

She caught my gaze and gave me a small, reassuring smile.

I liked her instantly.

"Do you ever go to bed hungry, sweetheart?"

For reference, this lady was a physical mixture of Miss Trunchbull from *Matilda* and Principal Mullins from

School of Rock. Her attitude was very on par with Nurse Ratched from *One Flew Over the Cuckoo's Nest.*

I blinked at her. *"No, ma'am."*

"Do you ever feel like you don't get enough food?"

I shook my head. *"Mama makes big dinners."*

And it was true. Our fridge was always stocked. Mom and Dad made sure we had everything we needed. My siblings ate just fine—*they* didn't collapse in the heat. But to the school and to these people, my condition looked like neglect.

From the kitchen, I could hear my mother's voice, tight with frustration. *"So let me get this straight—y'all think I don't feed my baby?"*

"We're just following up on a report from the school, ma'am," the older woman said coolly. *"Your daughter fainted, and her teacher said she was concerned about possible neglect."*

Mama let out a short, bitter laugh. *"Neglect?* **Neglect?!** *Do y'all know how **hot** it is outside? That baby didn't faint because she's hungry—she fainted because she can't sweat!"*

I sat frozen on the couch, my stomach twisted into knots. I had never seen Mama this angry before.

My father, who had been sitting quietly at the table, finally spoke up. *"I know exactly what this is about,"* he said, his voice low. *"This is about that 'Good Times' episode, isn't it?"*

There was a beat of silence.

The younger woman tilted her head. *"Excuse me?"*

Daddy leaned forward, folding his arms. *"That episode about Penny—how she was getting beat by her mama, and nobody noticed until she got burned with an iron. I bet you anything some school administrator saw that and decided they weren't about to 'miss the signs' again."*

Mama scoffed. *"Now every time a Black child so much as sneezes wrong, y'all think we abusing them."*

I didn't understand everything they were saying, but I knew exactly what *"Good Times"* was. It was one of the shows my parents liked to watch, and I had seen the episode they were talking about.

Penny, the little girl played by Janet Jackson, had a mother who hit her, locked her in closets, and eventually burned her with an iron. It was scary. It was heartbreaking.

And now, because of that episode, my parents were sitting in our own living room being treated like criminals.

The older CPS lady pursed her lips. *"Mr. and Mrs. Flowers, we are not here to judge you. We just need to verify that your children are safe and well cared for."*

Daddy shook his head. *"Well, look around. Our kids are*

fine. There's food in the kitchen, a roof over their heads. What more do you need to see?"

The younger woman glanced at me again. *"Lily, sweetheart, can I ask you a few questions?"*

I swallowed hard. *"Okay."*

She sat on the couch beside me, her voice kind. *"Are you ever left home alone for long periods of time?"*

I shook my head. *"No, ma'am."*

"Do you always have food to eat?"

"Yes, ma'am."

"Does anyone in your family ever hurt you?"

"No, ma'am."

She studied me for a moment, then nodded, jotting something down on her notepad. *"Alright. Thank you."*

The older woman sighed, snapping her folder shut. *"Well, everything appears to be in order. We'll close out the report."*

Mama crossed her arms. *"Good. Y'all wasted enough time as it is."*

They left a few minutes later, the younger woman offering Mama and Daddy a polite nod as she followed her partner out the door.

As soon as they were gone, Mama let out a long breath, shaking her head. *"I cannot believe this."*

Daddy muttered, *"All because of some TV show."*

I didn't say anything. I just sat there, my hands curled into my lap, trying to process what had just happened.

I had always thought that teachers were supposed to help kids, to make them feel safe. But today, it felt like my school had turned on me.

And for the first time, I realized—being different wasn't just hard.

It was dangerous.

It took weeks—*weeks*—before they finally left us alone. The caseworker eventually admitted there was no evidence of neglect. My pediatrician even wrote a letter explaining that I was being evaluated for a medical condition. But the damage had already been done.

My parents were furious. My mama, who had always been patient and kind, now had a sharp edge to her voice whenever she talked about the school. My daddy, who usually let Mom do most of the talking, was now the first to demand answers from my doctors, pushing harder than ever for someone to *"do something"* about what was happening to me.

As for me, I felt something new, something I didn't know how to name at the time.

Shame.

Not because of the investigation. Not because strangers had come into my house and treated my parents like criminals.

But because my body had made people question the people who loved me most. Because I had collapsed, and suddenly, my family had to *prove* that they were taking care of me.

I was only five years old, but I understood one thing clearly: my condition wasn't just hard on me. It was hard on everyone. And no matter how much I wanted to be like the other kids, no matter how much I tried to push through it… my body would always betray me.

We went to doctor after doctor, each one asking the same questions, running the same tests. No one had any real answers. Some said I needed to drink more water. Some thought it was low blood sugar. But I knew that wasn't it. None of their explanations made sense.

And the worst part? Half the time, it didn't even feel like they were really listening.

We'd sit in those cold exam rooms, me swinging my legs off the crinkly paper-covered table, Mom and Dad sitting nearby, their faces tight with frustration. A doctor would walk in, glance at my chart, and skim through our concerns like we were just another set of worried parents and a dramatic kid.

One doctor, an older man with a tired voice and a stethoscope slung lazily around his neck, barely looked up from his clipboard before shrugging. *"Some kids just don't sweat much,"* he said, like that was supposed to explain why I was collapsing outside. *"She's probably just a little sensitive to the heat. Maybe she needs to toughen up a bit."*

Toughen up. Like I was just being "soft." Like my body shutting down wasn't a medical issue—just a personal failing.

Then there was the woman who gave my mom a long, knowing look and said, *"Are you sure she's getting enough fresh air? Kids need to play outside, you know. It helps build their endurance."*

Endurance? *"Endurance?"* I wasn't out of shape. I wasn't weak because I spent too much time indoors. I was passing out because my body *couldn't* cool itself. But she said it like we were just another Black family keeping our kid inside, letting her play too many video games, like we needed her to tell us how to raise a child.

Then came the food lectures.

"You should really cut down on junk food. Processed snacks, fast food—it can cause all sorts of imbalances in the body. Try cooking more meals from scratch, something with real nutrients."

The irony of that one nearly made my mother come unglued. She cooked homemade meals almost every night. We had a fridge full of vegetables, fresh meats, leftovers from Sunday dinner. My siblings and I didn't survive on drive-thru meals and sugary snacks, but the doctor didn't know that. He didn't *ask.* He just assumed.

And the worst? The absolute most ridiculous suggestion?

"This might sound silly, but have you tried haircuts? A lot of little girls overheat because their hair traps heat against their scalp. Keeping it short could really help."

Mama's mouth had gone tight at that one. My hair had nothing to do with it. It wasn't some thick, smothering blanket trapping heat in my skull. But sure—let's just chop it all off and see if that magically fixes my broken sweat glands.

It was exhausting. Every appointment felt like a waste of time.

My father, who usually kept his temper in check, started getting more aggressive in his questioning. *"Are you even listening to us? We're telling you that she is collapsing from heat, that she does **not** sweat, and you're talking to us about junk food and haircuts?"*

And every time we left another office with no answers, I could feel the tension in my parents' shoulders tighten. I could hear it in the way my mother sighed when we got back in the car, in the way my father clenched the steering wheel just a little too hard.

The truth was, they weren't taking us seriously. They didn't see a medical mystery that needed solving—they saw a Black family they could dismiss with lazy, half-hearted advice.

And all the while, my body kept betraying me.

Then we met Dr. Carter.

She was different from the others. She didn't rush through the appointment or brush off my parents' concerns. She listened—really listened. She asked me questions in a way that made me feel like she actually cared.

After a long pause, she leaned forward and said, *"I believe Lily has anhidrosis."*

I didn't know what that meant, but the way Mom's fingers tightened around mine told me it wasn't good.

Dad repeated the word. *"Anhidrosis? He sounded like he was trying to piece it together. "What does that mean?"*

Dr. Carter folded her hands on the desk. *"It means Lily's body doesn't produce sweat. The sweat glands are either underdeveloped, damaged, or missing entirely. It's rare, but it can be dangerous—especially in extreme heat."*

I looked at Mom, waiting for her to tell me it was fine. That everything was going to be okay. But for the first time, I saw fear in her eyes.

"Is there a cure?" she asked.

Dr. Carter hesitated.

I held my breath.

"*No*," she finally said. "*But there are ways to manage it. Lily will need to be careful—avoid overheating, stay hydrated, and use external cooling methods when necessary.*"

I felt like the air had been sucked out of the room.

No cure.

No way to fix it.

Just careful.

In that moment, I realized that being different wasn't always a good thing.

———

CHAPTER THREE

SOCIAL ISOLATION

B y the time I reached the fifth grade, fainting wasn't new to me.

It had happened enough times that I lost count. The first time was at a Fourth of July barbecue when I was four. After that, it happened during a birthday party, at the state fair, even once in the parking lot after church. The worst part was that I never knew when it would happen. Sometimes I felt it coming—the sluggish heaviness, the way my skin burned like it was on fire from the inside. Other times, I wouldn't even have time to sit down before the world went black.

By now, my family, teachers, and even some classmates knew the routine. If I felt too hot, I had to stop whatever I was doing and find a way to cool down—water, shade, or air conditioning. But knowing what to do didn't make it any easier.

The cafeteria walk was proof of that.

When I was in kindergarten, the cafeteria had been all the way across the football field. That long stretch of sun and concrete was torture. Now, in fifth grade, the cafeteria wasn't as far, but it was still a hike. One that I hated.

And as you can imagine, lunchtime was the worst part of the day.

It wasn't the food—I actually liked the cafeteria's spaghetti and meatballs. It wasn't the noise either; I had five siblings, so loud chatter didn't bother me.

Per usual, it was the walk.

Even in early fall, outside felt like an oven, and our cafeteria was basically still clear across the campus. Most days, I barely made it before the world started spinning. My teachers knew by now to let me walk ahead so I could take my time, but that didn't stop the other kids from noticing.

When I was younger, kids would ask innocent questions. *"Why don't you play tag with us?"* or *"Why do you always go inside early?"* They weren't being mean—they were just curious. But by fifth grade, curiosity had turned into something else.

"Why you always walking so slow?"

"Lily's just lazy."

"Bet she's faking to get out of P.E."

"You think she's special or something?"

"She's just trying to get attention."

I tried not to let the words get to me, but they did. Every insult chipped away at me, little by little. I had read that bullying could damage your self-esteem, and I was starting to understand why.

Not in a textbook way. For the longest time, I didn't even really know what *"self-esteem"* was supposed to mean, not in a psychological sense, anyway. I just knew how I *felt*.

At home, around my family, I felt normal. My brothers and sisters never made me feel different. If we played outside, they already knew I couldn't last long, so they let me be the judge during races instead of forcing me to run. If we were walking somewhere and I needed to slow down, one of them would hang back and walk with me, just so I wouldn't be alone. My mom and dad never acted like I was a burden. They watched me closely, always made sure I stayed cool, but they never made a big deal about it.

Around them, I was just Lily.

But at school? Around children who *didn't* understand?

That's when I felt small.

Like I was shrinking inside myself, becoming less of who I used to be.

Years ago, I used to talk a lot. I was the kind of kid who asked a hundred questions in a row, just because I wanted to know everything. I liked telling stories, making people laugh, and raising my hand in class because I knew the answer.

But little by little, that part of me started disappearing.

Now, I hesitated before I spoke. What if I said something that made people think I was weird? What if they laughed at me? What if they thought I was faking again?

I started keeping my stories to myself. Keeping my questions in my head. Keeping my hand down, even when I knew the answer. It was easier that way. The more I kept to myself, the less attention I drew. And the less attention I drew, the less people had to say about me.

That was self-esteem, I realized. Not a definition from a dictionary. Not something from a psychology book. Just... how I felt.

Then one day, everything clicked—I *was* changing, shrinking into someone I barely recognized, and it wasn't just in my head. I came across the words, *"self-esteem"* in a magazine—*"Highlights for Children"*, I think. I liked flipping through it in the school library when my class went for reading time. There was an article about bullying, about how kids who got picked on sometimes started believing the things people said about them. That they were weak. That they weren't good enough. That something was wrong with them. It said bullying takes a toll on the victims self-esteem.

I remember staring at that page for a long time.

It was the first time I saw words that explained exactly how

I felt.

To make matters worse, the article was about younger kids. It didn't even talk about middle school bullies; the ones I was sure were going to be *way* worse than the ones I dealt with now.

Sixth grade was coming fast, and I wasn't ready.

I already knew what kids my age were capable of. I had a feeling the ones ahead of me—the ones who thought they were grown just because they were in middle school—wouldn't hold back.

Would they just tease me? Or would it be worse than that?

I tried not to think about it, but the closer summer got, the more I worried.

And the smaller I felt.

I hadn't told anyone yet, but I was absolutely dreading sixth grade. In my city, sixth grade meant middle school, and middle school had a reputation. According to my siblings, the older kids weren't just meaner—they were cruel. There were no more patient teachers watching over recess, no more familiar classmates I'd known since kindergarten. If I couldn't handle the teasing now, how would I survive next year?

I could already picture it. The whispers. The rumors. The names.

Faker. Liar. Weirdo.

And I didn't have to just picture it for long—because it was already happening.

It started small. Quick glances exchanged between classmates when I walked by, quiet snickers when I sat out during recess. But then it got worse. There's something about a child aging from 9 years old to 10 years old that just didn't add up when it comes to being unkind.

One afternoon, as I walked back from the water fountain, I noticed a group of kids huddled together near the library, sneaking looks in my direction. As soon as I passed, one of them bent down to tie their shoe. Then another. Then another.

Initially, I didn't get it.

Then I heard the laughter.

They were mocking me. Making fun of the way I had to squat down when I felt dizzy, the way I had to pause in the middle of walks just to keep from fainting.

There I was, tears prickling in my eyes, feeling smaller than I ever had before.

I wanted to disappear. Not just from that moment, not just from the teasing—but from everything. I was tired of always being the one left out, the one whispered about, the one who never quite fit anywhere. It wasn't just the heat that made my chest feel tight—it was the loneliness.

I had no one.

I watched the other kids move together so easily, laughing, nudging each other, forming bonds without even trying. I wasn't a part of that. I never had been. No one saved a seat for me at lunch. No one asked if I wanted to come over after school. No one included me in the jokes or the group chats or the secret notes passed under desks.

It was like I existed in a different world. One that ran parallel to everyone else's but never quite touched.

What hurt the most was that I had stopped expecting that to change.

I learned to brace myself every time I walked into a room, knowing the whispers might start up again. I knew which hallways to avoid, which corners of the playground were safest, which teachers would pretend not to hear the teasing. I had trained myself to keep my head down, to swallow the lump in my throat, to pretend I didn't care.

But I did.

I *did* care.

And no matter how much I told myself to be strong, to ignore them, to push through—I was tired.

So, so tired.

But if there was one thing I could always count on, it was the rain.

The worst bullies—the loudest ones, the meanest ones— *hated* rainy days. They whined when their socks got wet, complained about their hair frizzing up, and grumbled when recess got moved inside.

But me?

I *loved* it.

Rainy days made the world quieter. Softer. On those days, I didn't have to watch my classmates running across the playground without me. I didn't have to sit on the sidelines and pretend I didn't care. For once, we were all in the same place, moving at the same pace.

And on those days, I didn't feel small at all.

It was field day, and I already knew I wouldn't be able to participate. Mom had written a note, and my teacher promised I could stay inside instead of standing outside all day. But someone must have forgotten, because when my class lined up to go out, I was stuck in line with them.

"She just doesn't wanna lose," a boy named Roger muttered as we walked toward the field.

"She probably just don't wanna sweat," another kid laughed. *"Oh, wait. She can't."*

I bit my lip.

I wanted to say something. I wanted to yell that I wasn't

faking, that I would give anything to be able to run and play like them. But the words stuck in my throat.

Then, just as I was about to break away and tell my teacher, a voice cut in.

"Leave her alone."

I turned and saw Maya standing next to me. She was in my class, but we had never really talked before. She wasn't the loudest kid, but when she spoke, people listened.

That was the thing about Maya—she never had to raise her voice to be heard. She just had this way of saying things that made people stop and pay attention. I had noticed that about her early in the year. Even though we weren't exactly friends, I had noticed a lot of things about Maya.

Like the fact that we had the same favorite color—mauve. I saw her wearing it all the time, but I knew for certain because one day, we had to fill out an "About Me" worksheet for class, and when we exchanged papers to grade each other's work, I saw it written neatly in the blank space beside "Favorite Color: Mauve". I remember staring at it for a second, feeling oddly surprised. Most kids picked blue or red or purple—normal colors. But mauve? That was different. That was *my* favorite color.

And then there was the piano thing.

Maya took piano lessons—I was sure of that, too. Not because she ever said anything, but because I had caught her doing the same thing I always did when I was bored or nervous: playing an invisible piano on her desk. Her fingers would move across the surface like she was pressing real keys, pausing in between like she was listening to a song only she could hear. I did that all the time.

We had other things in common, too. We were both top students—two of the few kids who actually got excited about classwork, even when other people groaned. And she wore thick glasses, the kind that made her eyes look a little too big behind the lenses. I used to wonder if people teased her for them, *and the thick black strap she had securing them to her head,* the way they teased me for not sweating, but if they did, she didn't seem to care.

Maya didn't shrink under people's words. She didn't try to disappear.

And now, here she was, standing up for *me.*

Roger rolled his eyes. *"We're just joking."*

"Well, it's not funny," Maya shot back. *"You don't know what it's like to have something wrong with you."*

For a second, nobody said anything. Then, the teacher called for everyone to quiet down, and the teasing stopped—for now.

Maya walked beside me as we made our way to the field. *"You okay?"* she asked.

I nodded, but something inside me felt lighter.

Maybe I wasn't so alone after all.

Summer was supposed to be a break. A time to sleep in, ride bikes with my siblings, and watch cartoons all morning.

But that summer, I didn't feel like doing any of those things.

All I could think about was middle school.

I had already spent all of fifth grade worrying about it, but as the first day inched closer, my fear grew until it was all I could think about. I imagined the older kids pointing at me, whispering, laughing. Would they call me a liar, just like some of my classmates had? Would they make fun of me every time I had to sit out of gym? Would I have to explain myself over and over again, only for people to still not believe me?

What if they *did* believe me—but teased me anyway?

What if it got worse?

Every time I thought about it, my stomach twisted into knots. At first, I thought it was just nerves. But as the days passed, the knots got tighter. Sometimes, it was a dull ache that wouldn't go away, no matter how much I curled into myself. Other times, it was sharp and sudden, like someone was squeezing my insides.

By the time middle school was only three weeks away, I couldn't ignore it anymore.

Mom noticed first. *"Lily, you barely touched your breakfast,"* she said one morning. *"Something wrong?"*

I shook my head. *"I'm just not hungry."*

But the truth was, I *was* hungry. I just couldn't eat without feeling sick.

That night, the pain got worse. It started as a dull ache, then turned into a burning sensation in my stomach that made me curl up in bed, gripping my middle and biting my lip to keep from crying. I didn't want to wake anybody up, but my sister heard me shifting under the covers. She went to go get my mom.

"Baby, what's wrong?" she asked, flipping on the light.

I hesitated. *"My stomach."*

She sat beside me and rested a hand on my forehead, then my belly. *"Does it hurt when I press here?"*

I nodded.

It was bad enough that by the next morning, she was making an appointment.

Two days later, I was sitting in a doctor's office, swinging my feet over the edge of the exam table while a man in a white coat asked me a bunch of questions.

"Have you been eating normally?"

"No."

"Any nausea?"

"Sometimes."

"Do certain foods make it worse?"

I shrugged. It didn't seem to matter *what* I ate.

Finally, after pressing around my stomach and looking over some test results, he sighed. *"Lily, I think your stomach is producing too much acid. It's common in people who are under a lot of stress. If it keeps up, it could lead to ulcers."*

Ulcers? I was barely *eleven*!

Mom asked him what we could do. He prescribed me some medication to help reduce the acid and told me to avoid foods that could make it worse—spicy things, greasy things, anything too acidic.

But before we left, he said something else. *"The best thing Lily can do is find ways to relax. If she keeps worrying like this, the medicine won't be enough."*

When we got home, Mom gave me the pills, then sat beside me on the couch. She didn't say much at first, just rubbed my back while I stared at the TV without really watching it.

Finally, she sighed. *"You can't make yourself sick worrying about things that ain't even happened yet, baby."*

I wanted to tell her she didn't understand. That I *knew* something bad was going to happen, even if she didn't think so.

But I was too tired to argue.

The night before the first day of school in our house was always a little chaotic. This night, it rained.

Not just a drizzle—the kind of summer storm that made the air smell fresh and clean, that filled the ditches with water and turned the streets dark and shiny.

To help me calm down, my siblings had been talking about middle school all week, telling me everything they thought I needed to know—what teachers were nice, which hallways were impossible to get through, and how fast I had to move if I wanted to beat the lunch line rush. I had heard so much about it that I felt like I had already been there. But now, it was finally happening for *me*.

The whole house smelled like hair grease and shampoo. My sisters took turns sitting between mom's legs while she braided their hair, making sure their parts were straight and neat. My brothers had already gotten their fresh cuts earlier that day, and they kept running to the mirror, rubbing their heads and checking their line-ups like they were famous or something.

Everyone had their outfits picked out, neatly laid on their beds—brand new jeans, bright white sneakers that wouldn't stay clean past lunch, and backpacks still stiff from the store.

And, like every year, we had our pizza night.

Dad brought home two big pepperoni pizzas, but I stuck to the breadsticks. No pizza sauce for me—not with my stomach still getting back to normal. But even without the sauce, it was good.

We all squeezed onto the couch, passing plates back and forth while we watched *"The Toy"*—that funny movie with Richard Pryor and the rich kid who got everything he wanted. It always made us laugh, no matter how many times we watched it.

By the time the credits rolled, my stomach felt full but not sick, and for the first time all summer, I felt something close to excitement.

———

It was almost midnight. I sat by my bedroom window, watching the raindrops streak down the glass. The steady *tap, tap, tap* against the roof was one of the only sounds in the house. My siblings had all gone to bed, but I couldn't sleep. My stomach still felt a little bit tight, even with the medicine. My head was filled with too many thoughts, too many worries.

But as I watched the rain, I felt something shift inside me.

I had always loved the rain. Outside of our household, nobody else ever understood why. On rainy days, I felt like I could breathe easier, like I wasn't carrying a heavy weight on my chest. Maybe it was because, for once, *everybody* had to stay inside. I wasn't the odd one out, sitting in the shade while everyone else coexisted with the sun.

In the rain, I was just like everybody else.

As I pressed my forehead against the cool glass, I let out a slow breath.

Maybe the rain was a sign.

Maybe everything in middle school was going to be okay.

I wanted to believe it.

I *needed* to believe it.

Because tomorrow, it was finally happening.

Tomorrow, I would walk into middle school for the first time.

———————

CHAPTER FOUR

MIDDLE & HIGH SCHOOL

The moment I stepped into the middle school hallway, I knew everything had changed.

The voices were louder, the hallways more chaotic, and the students... bigger. The fifth graders had warned us about this—how the sixth graders were basically invisible, shoved out of the way while the seventh and eighth graders ruled the halls. I was already used to feeling small, but now, I felt microscopic.

And it didn't take long for me to realize that the teasing I had experienced in elementary school had been *nothing* compared to what was coming.

The whispering started immediately. I felt my ears burn as the comments circled around me like vultures.

"That's so weird."

"Wait, so she just never sweats? Like, ever?"

"What, is she some kind of robot?"

I kept my head down, pretending to focus on the floor, but my stomach twisted into knots.

It was happening all over again.

By second period, I had already been a Social Studies class highlight.

"Hey, aren't you the girl who can't sweat?" one boy asked loudly as I slid into my seat.

I didn't answer, but that didn't matter.

Someone else jumped in. *"Yeah, she fakes being sick all the time so she don't have to do gym."*

By now, I had enough medical proof to back me up—doctor's notes, test results, letters from specialists explaining my condition in words far too complicated for most kids to understand. The school *knew* I wasn't making it up. The teachers *knew* I physically couldn't overheat without serious consequences. Hell, even *the state* knew!

So, I had been officially excused from participating in gym class.

But that didn't mean I got to sit out completely.

Instead of running laps or playing dodgeball, I was still expected to "dress out" like everyone else—swap my regular clothes for the stiff, oversized gym uniform that clung to my skin in the worst way. And after that, I basically became the designated helper for the gym teacher.

Some days, I kept score during basketball games. Other days, I handed out equipment or helped pick up cones after drills. If there was a written test, I passed out the papers. If someone forgot their water bottle, I was the one sent to grab an extra from the office.

It wasn't the worst thing in the world.

But it wasn't the best, either.

Because no matter how official my medical excuse was, no matter how many doctors confirmed that I *couldn't* participate, the teasing never stopped.

"She just don't wanna sweat her hair out."

*"Bet she could run if she **wanted** to."*

"Must be nice, getting to sit on the sidelines while the rest of us suffer."

Like I had *chosen* this. Like I wouldn't have given *anything* to be able to run and play like them.

But they didn't care about that.

They only cared about what they *thought* was true.

———

I met Jimmy early in sixth grade, before every day started to feel like a struggle for survival. He wasn't in my homeroom, but we had gym together—if you could even call it that for me. While the other kids ran laps, I stood on the sidelines, tallying scores and collecting basketballs when they rolled out of bounds. That's how we first started talking.

"You're lucky," he said one day, plopping down on the bleachers beside me. He was out of breath, sweaty from running, but grinning like he had just won a gold medal. *"Coach nearly killed us with those sprints."*

I gave a small shrug. *"I'd trade places with you if I could."*

He laughed like I was joking, but I wasn't.

Jimmy was different from the other kids. He didn't mock me or ask stupid questions about why I didn't sweat. He just talked to me—about video games, about his dog that had recently chewed through his mom's favorite purse, about the time his older brother convinced him that eating a raw onion would make him stronger. He made me laugh. For the first time in what felt like forever, I had someone to sit with during lunch, someone who made school a little less unbearable.

And then there was that afternoon in the rain.

It was late October, and a sudden downpour had trapped a group of us under the awning outside the school's gym. Buses were running late, and most kids grumbled about getting their new shoes wet. But not me.

The rain called to me.

I stood at the edge of the overhang, watching the fat drops hit the pavement, feeling the cool mist against my face. I wanted to step out into it, let the water soak through my clothes, cool my skin in a way nothing else ever could.

Jimmy must have noticed the look on my face because he nudged me with his elbow. *"You love the rain, huh?"*

I hesitated, embarrassed. *"Yeah."*

"Huh." He tilted his head. *"It **is** kinda nice."*

And just like that, he stepped out into the downpour.

For a second, I couldn't believe it. Jimmy—who cared way too much about his sneakers and always complained when his socks got wet—was standing in the middle of the rain, arms outstretched like he was soaking in the moment.

I laughed. A real, full laugh.

He turned back to me. *"Come on, Lily."*

I didn't need to be told twice. I stepped off the curb and joined him, feeling the water trickle down my face, drench my clothes, cool my skin. It was one of the few times I felt like *me*—not the girl who couldn't sweat, not the weird kid on the sidelines, just a kid standing in the rain with her friend.

But middle school friendships were fragile.

By the time seventh grade started, things had changed.

Jimmy still waved when he saw me, still smiled in the hallways—but it wasn't the same. He stopped sitting with me at lunch. Stopped walking with me to class. Stopped talking to me unless we were forced to work together on something.

At first, I thought I had done something wrong.

But then I overheard his friends.

"Why do you even talk to her?" one of them scoffed. *"She's weird."*

"Yeah," another one added. *"She just stands around during gym like she's too good to do anything."*

Jimmy didn't argue. He didn't defend me. He just stood there, silent.

That hurt worse than anything.

It was easier when kids were outright mean—when they mocked me, whispered about me, rolled their eyes at my medical excuse. At least then, I knew where I stood. But Jimmy had been my friend. He had *chosen* to talk to me, to laugh with me, to stand in the rain like it was the best thing in the world.

And now?

Now, he was too afraid to be seen with me.

That's when I started thinking about Maya again.

Maya, who had stood next to me in fifth grade when I felt like the whole world was against me. Maya, who never once made me feel like I had to explain myself. Maya, who had been *there* for me.

I hadn't spoken to her since elementary school, but I wondered about her constantly. Did she like middle school? Did she make new friends? Did she ever think about me?

I longed for a friendship like that again.

But middle school wasn't so kind.

At some point in grade seven, I stopped thinking about Maya.

She had been in my life for such a short time, just long enough to stand up for me when I needed it, just long enough to make me think—*maybe*—I could have a real friend. But then she was gone.

On the last day of school she had told everyone her family was moving away to a different state that summer. And so, I assumed that was it. She had moved on to a new town, a new school, a new life.

So when I saw her walking through the hall in eighth grade, I thought I was imagining things.

She was taller now, her glasses a little different, her hair pulled into a neat bun. But it was *her.*

For a moment, I thought about saying something. About calling her name. But then I hesitated. What if she didn't remember me? What if she had forgotten all about that day in fifth grade?

But then—just as I was about to turn away—our eyes met.

And she smiled.

I blinked, startled.

Then, slowly, I smiled back.

Later that day, Maya found me in the library.

"*You disappeared,*" I said before I could stop myself.

She laughed. "*So did you.*"

I frowned. "*I thought you moved.*"

She sighed, shifting her books. "*We were supposed to. My parents had a whole plan—new jobs, a new house, the whole thing. But at the last minute, the plans fell through. We couldn't afford to go, so we stayed.*"

I stared at her. "*You've been here **this whole time?!**"*

Maya nodded. "*I was at the other middle school on the north side. My parents thought it would be a better fit, but I hated it. I was so excited to finally start middle school with you, and when we didn't move, I thought—maybe—we'd still get to be friends. But then, we weren't at the same school."*

I swallowed. *"I didn't even know."*

She sighed. *"I thought about finding you. But then I started hearing things. People talking about you, about the stuff they said in elementary school. I figured... maybe you didn't want a friend who reminded you of all that."*

I opened my mouth, but nothing came out.

How had we spent *years* at separate schools, both wishing for the same thing, both too afraid to look in a phone book and reach out?

But none of that mattered now.

Because Maya was here.

And for the first time in a long time, I felt like maybe—I wasn't completely alone.

———

Maya and I didn't become best friends overnight.

But little by little, we started talking again. Sitting together in class. Partnering up for projects. It wasn't like the friendships I saw other girls have—braiding each other's hair, sharing secrets about crushes and weekend plans.

But it was something.

We spent a lot of time in the library and in the courtyard during our lunch hour talking and catching up on all the things we were doing since elementary school graduation. I had to let her know that my first year of middle school was a battlefield. Not just because of the teasing—but because of all the ways I was left out.

Seventh grade brought school dances, and I never got asked to one. My classmates paired off, giggling about who liked who, who kissed who behind the gym after school. But me? I was invisible.

And as I sat with her at lunch one day, listening to her talk about a piano recital she was preparing for, I felt something I hadn't felt in years.

Hope.

Maybe my pre-teenage years hadn't been what I wanted them to be. Maybe I had been left out of the dances and the parties and the first kisses.

But maybe… just maybe… things were starting to change.

I had only one more year to go, but thankfully, I wasn't fighting it alone.

Not anymore.

Maya was here. She had come back into my life when I least expected it, and unlike Jimmy, she wasn't afraid to be seen with me. If anything, she made it *her mission* to remind me that I had just as much right to be here as anyone else.

For the Homecoming dance, I didn't even have time to feel left out.

"*You know what?*" Maya had said, tossing the crumpled dance flyer into the trash without hesitation. "*I don't even want to go. I heard the DJ last year was trash.*"

"*You don't have to skip just because of me,*" I had mumbled.

"*I know,*" she said simply. "*But I want to.*"

And that was that.

Instead of sitting in a sweaty gym, watching everyone else twirl around under dim lighting, we went to the library and spent the evening quizzing each other on random trivia. Maya's confidence was unwavering—she had no problem rejecting something that wasn't meant for her, and her refusal to shrink herself made me wonder if maybe… I didn't have to either.

Eighth grade brought field trips and pep rallies. The heat during outdoor events was unbearable, so I always had to sit in the shade or stay inside. But this time, I wasn't alone.

"*The sun is overrated,*" Maya declared, plopping down next

to me under the covered pavilion while the rest of our class screamed in the bleachers at the pep rally. *"And besides, I wouldn't even **see** half the game. You **know** I can't see three feet in front of me without my glasses."*

She pushed them up her nose for emphasis, the thick lenses magnifying her eyes in a way that should have made her self-conscious. But it didn't.

Maya couldn't hide her poor vision even if she wanted to—everyone knew about it. They saw how thick her glasses were, how she had to squint without them, how she struggled in gym class because she refused to wear her glasses during dodgeball. And yet, none of it stopped her from standing tall, from speaking up, from looking people in the eye without flinching.

I envied that about her.

Ninth grade brought Friday night football games and bonfires. But I wasn't invited.

Maya was.

"You going?" I had asked, trying not to sound bitter.

She rolled her eyes. *"Absolutely not."*

I frowned. *"Why?"*

"Because I already know how that's going to go," she said, counting off on her fingers. *"One: It'll be crowded and loud. Two: I won't be able to see a single thing on the field.*

Three: You're my only friend that actually talks about real stuff, and I don't want to waste a Friday listening to people pretend to care about a game they don't understand."

I laughed. *"That's the nerdiest thing I've ever heard."*

She smirked. *"Exactly. Now, let's go get ice cream instead."*

And we did.

Tenth grade brought pool parties in the summer. The irony was, the one place where I actually felt comfortable—the water—was the one place I was excited to go.

But then it rained.

Hard.

The kind of summer storm that sent everyone running for cover, that quickly flooded the lowest parts of the yard and turned the sky dark and beautiful.

Maya and I were walking back from the library when it started.

People scrambled around us, ducking under awnings, pulling jackets over their heads, whining about their hair and shoes. But not me.

And not Maya.

Instead of running, we slowed down.

Maya tipped her head back, letting the rain soak her face. *"You know what?"* she said, voice full of quiet awe. *"This is actually kind of nice."*

I grinned. *"Told you."*

She turned to me. *"I get it now. Feels amazing! This is your thing, huh?"*

I nodded. "The only time I don't feel different is when it rains."

She studied me for a moment, then nodded, like she was taking that in, tucking it away for safekeeping.

We didn't rush home. We didn't try to escape it. We walked through the rain, letting it drench us, letting it wash away the weight of everything else.

Eleventh grade brought corny promposals and excitement over dresses and heels.

Maya got asked to prom.

I didn't.

I never expected to, but it still stung.

"I already know what you're about to say," I told her when she walked up to my locker, eyes narrowed in warning.

Maya smirked. *"Do you?"*

"You don't have to skip prom for me."

She folded her arms. *"Good, because I wasn't planning on skipping it. I was planning on taking you."*

I blinked. *"Wait... what?"*

"You heard me."

"But... I thought you got asked already?"

She shrugged. *"And? Who says I have to say yes? He didn't even ask me in a cool way. Just 'Hey, you wanna go to prom?' Like, sir. **Sir**. I deserve better than that."*

I laughed. *"So now I'm your backup plan?"*

"Nope. You were always Plan A."

She grabbed my hand and squeezed. *"So, what do you say? We get dressed up, make fun of people's bad dance moves, and show everyone what nerd royalty looks like?"*

I bit my lip, overwhelmed by how much this moment meant to me.

For once, I wasn't sitting on the sidelines, watching life pass me by.

I was about to be participating.

———————

Maya wasn't joking about prom.

The moment I said yes, she went into full planning mode. I had never seen her so determined—or so excited.

"We need dresses," she announced the next day at lunch, shoving a fashion magazine in front of me. *"Shoes. Makeup. The whole nine yards."*

I stared at the glossy pages, filled with pictures of girls in shimmering gowns, their hair styled in perfect curls. It felt like a world I didn't belong to—until now.

"Lily," Maya said, grinning, *"we're about to shut this prom down."*

I laughed, shaking my head. *"You really think so?"*

"I know so." She adjusted her thick glasses and leaned in, lowering her voice dramatically. *"For too long, these people have underestimated us. They don't know what's coming."*

It was the first time I had ever been excited about something school-related. And it was all because of Maya.

A week before prom, Maya and I went dress shopping.

"I want something bold," she declared, flipping through the racks. *"Something that says, 'Yes, I'm a nerd, but I'm also **that girl.**'"*

I chuckled. *"I just want something that doesn't make me look ridiculous."*

We tried on dress after dress, twirling in front of the mirrors, rating each other's choices. After an hour, I found *the one*—a deep blue satin gown that hugged my figure in all the right ways. It wasn't flashy, but it was elegant. Classic. And for once, when I looked at myself, I didn't feel like I was fading into the background.

Maya found hers minutes later—a deep burgundy gown with a high slit and just enough sparkle to catch the light. *"This,"* she declared, spinning in front of the mirror. *"This is the dress that will make history."*

The night before prom, we had a "get ready" sleepover at Maya's house.

"We're doing the full experience," she said, lining up bottles of nail polish and makeup on her vanity. *"Hair, nails, facials—everything."*

I laughed as she slathered a face mask onto my skin. *"This is a lot of effort for people who have ignored us for years."*

*"This isn't for **them**,"* she corrected. *"This is for **us**."*

And she was right.

As she curled my hair, carefully pinning sections so the curls would hold, something inside me clicked into place. I was no longer the girl watching from the edges. I was right in the middle of the moment, where I was *supposed* to be.

Finally, I liked the girl in the mirror.

And I had Maya to thank for that.

Prom was *magical*.

The gym had been transformed with twinkling lights and elegant decorations that almost made us forget it was just a glorified basketball court. Music blasted through the speakers, kids were dressed in their best, and finally, I didn't feel like an outsider.

Maya and I had promised to have fun, and we *did*.

We danced like nobody was watching, laughing at the stiff, awkward moves of the people around us. We lip-synced dramatically to slow songs, made ridiculous poses in the photo booth, and stuffed our faces with fancy cupcakes from the refreshment table.

Some people looked at us like we were crazy. Others whispered behind their hands, like they couldn't believe we actually showed up. But this time, I didn't care.

Then, something unexpected happened.

I was mid-bite into my second cupcake when Maya nudged me. *"Hey. Guy at three o'clock. He's been staring at you for at least five minutes."*

I nearly choked. *"What? Who?"*

She subtly tilted her head toward a tall, broad-shouldered guy standing near the edge of the dance floor. He was dressed sharply in a navy blue suit, his tie slightly loosened like he had already danced a little too hard.

"Do you know him?" I asked, confused.

"Nope," Maya said. *"But he definitely knows you."*

Before I could overthink it, he made his way over.

"Hey," he said, flashing a crooked smile. *"I'm Marcus."*

"Uh... hi," I said, glancing at Maya.

He gestured toward the dance floor. *"You wanna dance?"*

I froze.

No boy had *ever* asked me to dance. Not once. I had spent years being invisible—how was this happening?

Maya's grin was so wide I thought her face might split. *"She would loooove to,"* she answered for me, practically pushing me toward him.

Marcus laughed. *"You've got a good friend."*

"The best," I agreed, letting him take my hand.

As we swayed to the music, I couldn't stop myself from blurting out, *"Why me?"*

Marcus raised an eyebrow. *"Why not you?"*

I blinked.

"I saw you and your friend having fun," he explained. *"You weren't trying to impress anyone. You weren't trying to be anyone but you. I liked that."*

I didn't know what to say.

So, I just danced.

After the song ended, Marcus and I ended up at a quiet table, talking like we had known each other forever. He told me he went to a different high school but was at our prom with his cousins. I told him about my love for the rain, and instead of looking at me like I was strange, he said, *"That's actually kind of beautiful."*

Maya, meanwhile, was watching from across the room, beaming like a proud parent.

When the night ended, Marcus asked for my number.

As I scribbled it down, I realized something: this was a turning point.

I wasn't just existing anymore.

I was *living*.

It was the first time I truly believed I deserved it.

Twelfth grade brought senior trips, senior skip days, and the excitement of leaving high school behind.

I wasn't just *that girl* anymore. The one people whispered about. The one who sat in the shade while everyone else played in the sun.

I still stood apart from the rest.

But I wasn't invisible.

I wasn't forgotten.

Because Maya and Marcus never let me be.

Since prom, my life had started to change in ways I never expected.

Marcus and I had fallen into an easy rhythm—late-night phone calls that stretched until my mom yelled at me to get off the line, weekend movie marathons where he let me pick the weirdest indie films I could find, and casual dates at the local diner where we shared fries and laughed about nothing and everything at the same time.

He made me feel comfortable in my own skin. I never had to explain myself to him, never had to shrink myself down or apologize for who I was. He accepted my quirks the same way Maya always had—like they were just parts of me, not things that made me *less*.

And Maya?

She was my biggest supporter.

When I told her about my first date with Marcus, she clutched her chest dramatically and said, *"My little nerd baby is growing up."*

"Stop," I groaned, shoving her playfully.

"I will not stop," she said proudly. *"This is a major life event! Who knew the awkward girl who hid in the shade all her life would have two people fighting for her attention?"*

I laughed, rolling my eyes. *"Nobody's fighting for me."*

She wagged her finger. *"Oh, but we are, Lily. Marcus and I? We're your personal fan club. And you better get used to it."*

And the truth was… I kind of loved it.

I found myself in the midst of my own quirks, leaning into the things that had once made me feel like an outsider.

I still loved the rain, but now I had people who loved it with me. When it stormed, Marcus and I would sit on his porch, watching the raindrops race down the wooden steps. He didn't mind getting wet. He just liked being there with me.

Maya and I still nerded out together, but now we did it *loudly*, without caring who heard. One time, we spent an entire lunch period debating which Hogwarts house I would be in (she was convinced I was a Ravenclaw; I argued for

Hufflepuff). By the time the bell rang, half our classmates were listening in—and for once, they weren't laughing *at* me. They were laughing *with* me.

I had never felt that before.

And I was still an overachiever, but now it wasn't something I tried to hide. Marcus would sit with me at the library, pretending to study but mostly just doodling in his notebook, watching me scribble furiously in mine. "*You're going to take over the world one day,*" he'd say with a grin.

And, I kind of believed him.

Maya never left my corner.

Sometimes, when I lay in bed at night, staring at the ceiling, I wondered if she was an angel God had sent just for me. She had come back into my life at exactly the right time, pulling me out of the shadows and into the light. She never let me fall too deep into self-doubt. She never let me forget that I mattered.

"*I don't think you understand how much you've done for me,*" I told her one afternoon.

We were lying on the grass in my backyard, watching the clouds drift by. She pushed her thick glasses up her nose and turned to look at me. "*What do you mean?*"

"*I mean...*" I exhaled, trying to put it into words. "*If you hadn't been my friend, I don't think I ever would've let anyone in. Not Marcus. Not anybody.*"

Maya snorted. *"Oh, please. You give me way too much credit."*

"No, I don't." I sat up, crossing my legs. *"You believed in me before I ever believed in myself. You taught me how to be myself."*

Maya rolled onto her stomach, propping her chin up with her hands. *"Well,"* she said with a smirk, *"I am pretty great."*

I laughed. *"Yeah. You are."*

She smiled softly. *"So are you."*

I was still different.

But now, that difference didn't feel like something I had to apologize for.

Marcus made me feel seen.

Maya made me feel strong.

And because of them, I felt included.

————

By the time I reached grade six, I had learned how to move through school without being noticed. But by the time I reached my high school graduation, Maya had taught me how to do the opposite.

To walk with my head held high.

To take up space.

To own my story.

And because of her love and support, I wasn't afraid to do any of that anymore.

Sometimes, if you're lucky, you find the kind of friend who makes you believe in yourself.

And sometimes, if you're really lucky, they stand in the rain with you.

———————

CHAPTER FIVE

FIRST GLIMPSE OF HOPE

I had spent my entire life learning how to exist in the heat without the one thing everyone else took for granted—sweat.

I had perfected the art of avoidance, seeking shade like my life depended on it. Because, in a way, it did. I knew exactly which hallways at school had the best air conditioning, which places had cold tile floors I could press my face against if I ever felt like I was about to pass out. I had trained myself to recognize the warning signs— when my skin started to burn from the inside, when my vision blurred just enough to tell me I needed to stop, sit, cool down before my body shut down entirely.

But despite everything I had learned, nothing had prepared me for what happened next.

It was the kind of heat that sat on your chest like a

boulder, pressing the air out of your lungs before you even had a chance to breathe it in.

I had woken up before the sun that morning, groggy and already dreading the long drive ahead. My job was an hour away, and the idea of making that commute in *July*, in *Louisiana*, in a *black car* with no air conditioning, was enough to make my stomach twist.

But I didn't have a choice.

I climbed into my Mitsubishi Galant—DeeDee, as I called her—and sighed as I turned the key. The engine rumbled to life, but the air conditioning? Dead.

I rolled down the windows, hoping the breeze would help. It didn't.

By the time I pulled out onto the road, the sun was beginning to creep up over the horizon, turning the sky into a soft orange glow. The temperature was already *96 degrees*. At 8 o'clock in the morning.

I had driven in uncomfortable heat before, but this was different. The car felt like a *furnace on wheels*, absorbing the heat and trapping it inside with me. The longer I drove, the worse it got. The hot wind whipping through the windows was useless—it didn't cool me down. It just made me feel like I was being *cooked* in my own car.

My clothes stuck to my skin. My arms were slick against the steering wheel. The seatbelt burned my collarbone. I was miserable, but I knew what to expect.

Or at least, I thought I did.

About halfway into my drive, I started feeling... off.

Not the usual *I'm-too-hot* kind of off. Something was different.

The heat was unbearable, yes, but I wasn't dizzy. My skin wasn't turning bright red like it usually did when I overheated. My head wasn't throbbing. I wasn't slipping into that terrifying fog of heat exhaustion that had haunted me my entire life.

Instead, I felt *wet*.

It was a slow realization. At first, I thought maybe I had spilled something, that maybe the bottle of water I kept in the passenger seat had leaked onto my back. Crazy, right? But then I shifted in my seat and felt it—

A dampness clinging to my shirt.

I reached behind me, fingers brushing against my lower back, and froze.

My shirt was soaked.

For the first time in my life, I was *sweating*.

———

I should have been disgusted. I should have been uncomfortable. Everyone always complained about sweating, about how gross it was, how it ruined their clothes, how it made them *feel sticky and dirty*.

But all I felt was pure, unfiltered *joy*.

A laugh bubbled up from my throat—half disbelief, half exhilaration. I gripped the steering wheel tighter, blinking against the shock of it all.

I had spent my whole life wondering if my body even *had* sweat glands. I had been poked and prodded by doctors, forced to hear their vague, unsure explanations about why I couldn't regulate my temperature like a normal person. And now, here I was, *soaked*, proof that my body wasn't completely broken.

I had them. I had sweat glands. They just didn't work *properly*.

The thought sent a chill down my spine, a stark contrast to the unbearable heat filling the car. If I could sweat under these extreme conditions, what did that mean?

Had my body just given up after years of failing me? Had I somehow tricked my broken internal thermostat into working?

Or worse—was this a one-time thing?

The excitement swirled into uncertainty. What if it never happened again? What if I got my hopes up, only for my body to betray me like it always had?

I couldn't let myself believe this was permanent.

Not yet.

When I finally pulled into the parking lot at work, I took a moment to gather myself. My body was drenched, my shirt clinging to my back, my hair damp at the roots. But instead of feeling exhausted like I usually did after overheating, I felt... regulated.

Like my body had *actually* tried to cool me down instead of letting me burn.

I sat there for a few more minutes, breathing heavily, waiting for the usual crash that came with getting too hot.

It never came.

I thought about all the years I had spent searching for answers, all the times I had felt like I was just *defective*. And now, it all made sense.

I didn't have a complete lack of sweat glands—I had a *broken thermostat*.

My body wasn't able to regulate itself properly. It went from normal, to *too hot*, to *too cold*, without any gradual transition. It wasn't that I *couldn't* sweat—it was that my brain wasn't sending the right signals *until it was almost too late*.

It had taken an extreme situation—an hour in a hot car, completely still, no breeze, no movement—to finally push my body past its limits. I was still cautious, still unsure of what this meant in the long run. But for the first time, I had something I had never had before.

Hope.

Still sitting the parking lot with my foot on the brake, I finally threw the car into park and grabbed my phone with shaky hands. My heart was still racing, my mind still spinning with disbelief. *I had sweat.* For the first time in my life, my body had done something I never thought it could do.

I needed to tell someone. *I needed to tell Maya.*

I pressed her name in my favorites list, bouncing my knee as the phone rang.

She picked up on the first ring. *"What's up, nerd?"*

"I sweat!" I practically yelled into the phone.

There was a beat of silence. Then—

"Wait. What?"

"I sweat," I repeated, breathless. *"Like, actual sweat. On my skin. From my body. Mine!"*

Maya sucked in a dramatic gasp. *"Oh my God! Where? How? What happened?"*

I launched into the story, telling her every detail about the brutal heat, about DeeDee turning into an oven, about the moment I realized my shirt was actually *wet*—not from a spilled drink, not from water, but from my own body.

She listened, completely silent, which was *rare* for Maya. Then she whispered, like she had just witnessed a miracle, *"Lily… you're human after all."*

I barked out a laugh, the kind that was half joy, half disbelief. *"I know, right? I seriously thought I didn't even have sweat glands."*

"This is huge." Her voice was firm, filled with that same unwavering confidence she always had when she talked me through my insecurities. "You *needed* this."

I swallowed the lump in my throat. *"Yeah. I really did."*

There was a long pause before she asked, softer now, *"How do you feel?"*

I stared out the windshield, watching the early morning sun shine through the trees standing tall over the pool facility. I had spent so much of my life feeling *defective*, like something in me was fundamentally broken. And now?

"I feel… hopeful."

Maya let out a little sniff. *"Oh, don't do that,"* she groaned. *"Don't go making me all emotional at nine in the morning."*

I laughed. *"You love it."*

"I do love it," she admitted. *"And I love you. And I love that your body is finally catching up to how awesome you*

are."

"*Thanks, Maya.*" I swallowed again, steadying myself. "*I should get inside.*"

"*Yeah, yeah,*" she sighed dramatically. "*Go be an important, rule-enforcing pool queen. I'll call you later.*"

I grinned. "*Talk soon.*"

I hung up, pressing the phone to my chest for a moment before exhaling.

Maya was the first person I called. But the next person I wanted to tell? *Marcus.*

I swiped to my messages and typed:

Lily: "*Hey, I have some good news to tell you later.*" A minute later, my phone vibrated.

Marcus: "*Good news, huh? Does this mean you finally admitted that I'm funnier than you?*"

I rolled my eyes, smiling.

Lily: "Absolutely not. I'll call you later, though."

Marcus: "Can't wait. Miss you, babe."

Lily: "Miss you too."

I stared at the message for a second, heart swelling in my chest.

Marcus and I had been officially together for a while now. Our relationship had settled into something comfortable— something *real*. We spent as much time together as we could, even with our college classes and part-time jobs getting in the way. Late-night phone calls, weekend study sessions at coffee shops, spontaneous drives just to talk about nothing and everything.

He made me feel normal. Not different. Not like an outsider. Just *Lily*.

I slipped my phone into my pocket, inhaled deeply, and stepped out of the car.

Time to start the day.

Here I was, still in a daze, the feeling of sweat on my back a lingering reminder that something incredible had just happened. But I couldn't focus on that now—I had a job to do.

A *big* job.

I wasn't just a lifeguard. I was *the* Head Lifeguard.

It wasn't something I had asked for.

When I had applied for the city's standard lifeguard position, I just wanted a summer job—something to keep me busy, earn some money, and, most importantly, keep me in the water, where my body felt the most comfortable. I had no expectations beyond that. But when it came time to test our skills, I didn't just *pass*—I dominated.

The city's lifeguard testing wasn't just about knowing how to swim. It was about knowing how to *save lives*.

The swim test was brutal.

Each applicant had to swim 500 meters nonstop—20 laps in an Olympic-sized pool—within a set time. It was supposed to separate the strong swimmers from the weak ones. Most struggled by lap 10, dragging themselves to the edge to rest before pushing off again.

But me?

I finished a full 16 minutes before the next closest person.

I had always been fast in the water, but even I hadn't realized how much faster I was until I saw the looks on their faces. Some of the veteran guards, the ones who had been working for years, stood on the pool deck watching. I could hear them murmuring.

"Who is she?"

"How is she still going?"

"She's not even tired!"

And that was just the beginning.

Passing the *American Red Cross Lifeguard Training Course* wasn't just about swimming fast—it was about proving you could save a life under the worst conditions.

The evaluators didn't make it easy.

For the deep-water rescue test, they had a *200-pound man*—a fully trained rescue dummy, weighted to simulate a real drowning victim—drop to the bottom of the deepest part of the pool, 12 feet below the surface.

Our job?

Swim to the victim, dive down, pull him up, and tow him 20 meters to safety—without touching the bottom.

One by one, the candidates attempted it. Some made it down but struggled to lift the weight back up. Some got the dummy to the surface but lost their grip halfway through the tow. Some just couldn't get past the sheer pressure of 12 feet of water pressing down on their lungs, while some barely made it halfway down before panicking altogether.

Then it was my turn.

I dove in, cutting through the water in a smooth, practiced motion. As I reached the bottom, I positioned myself, gripped the rescue dummy with both arms, and exploded off the pool floor with everything I had.

Breaking the surface, I rolled the "victim" onto my chest, keeping his head above water. Then, using only my legs, I powered through the 20-meter tow, keeping my strokes steady, my breath controlled.

By the time I reached the edge, the evaluators weren't just nodding. They were *clapping.* I wasn't even out of breath. They said they had *"never seen anything like it"*!

Once the final tests were over, the hiring team had made their decision unanimously—I wasn't just getting the job. I was getting *four* pools to oversee.

And that was how, despite being a first-year guard, I became Head Lifeguard and a Supervisor over four swimming pools—to the dismay of every veteran lifeguard who thought the position should've been theirs.

———————

Normally, I worked closer to home, but today was different.

I walked into work that morning, in shock. My mind was still turning over the events of the drive, still replaying Maya's excitement, Marcus's teasing text, the sheer amazement of realizing my body had done something it had never done before.

But as soon as I stepped onto the pool deck, my Head Lifeguard instincts kicked in.

This wasn't just any pool. *This was the pool.*

It was one of the city's most expensive facilities, located in an affluent neighborhood filled with people who had more money than patience. The kind of parents who *expected* their kids to be treated like royalty and weren't afraid to call the city office if they didn't get their way. And here I was—an *outsider*, the new "Head Lifeguard", a *first-year* worker promoted straight to the top.

I knew the other lifeguards still resented it. I could see it in their stiff nods, in the way they hesitated before following my orders. I had been *younger*, *newer*, and yet, I had been placed above them.

But it was a *them* problem, not mine. You know?

Today, I was here at the farthest pool, covering for a Lead Guard who had been injured. That meant driving an hour in the blazing heat, nearly passing out from heat exhaustion—only to walk onto a pool deck filled with lifeguards who still didn't respect me.

I shifted my folded towel under my arm and slung my red rescue tube over my shoulder, scanning the pool.

The lifeguards were all at their stations, some sitting in the high chairs, others standing at rotation points. None of them acknowledged me.

Fine.

Let them sulk.

I *earned* this position.

I was here to do a job.

And no rude looks were going to make me feel like I didn't belong.

Because I *did* belong.

Maya had spent years reminding me of that—pulling me out of the shadows, refusing to let me shrink myself just because other people couldn't handle my presence. She had taught me to stand tall, to own my space, to walk like I had every right to be here.

And I *did*.

So, as I adjusted my sunglasses and stepped across the pool deck, I didn't flinch at the cold stares. I didn't hesitate. I didn't shrink.

Instead, I walked with my head high, knowing exactly who I was.

Walking to my station, I scanned the glistening blue water, and settled into position.

It didn't matter what they thought of me.

———————

CHAPTER SIX

DEVELOPING RESILIENCE

Having anhidrosis wasn't just an inconvenience—it shaped nearly every aspect of my life.

People who could regulate their body temperature never had to think about it. They could step outside in the summer, jog from their car to a building, sit in the sun for a few minutes without consequence. They could overheat, sweat, cool down, and move on.

I couldn't.

For me, every choice, every plan, every mundane activity required strategy.

Going to an outdoor event? I had to check the weather obsessively, calculating how long I could last before the heat became dangerous.

Walking across a large parking lot? I had to mentally map out shaded spots along the way, in case I needed to stop.

Attending a wedding? I had to choose my seat carefully, making sure I was close to air conditioning or a fan.

Even something as simple as standing in line at a store could turn into a medical emergency if I wasn't careful.

People always said, *"Oh, not sweating is no big deal."* But if it wasn't a big deal, why did basically every other living creature on Earth do it?

I was tired of hearing it.

And I was even more tired of *having to explain myself.*

I had seen countless doctors over the years—some helpful, some dismissive. But when I found Dr. Whitaker, a dermatologist who actually *understood* anhidrosis, everything changed.

He didn't just look at me like some medical oddity. He understood exactly what I was going through.

"So," he said, tapping his pen against my file, *"I'm sure you already know this, but anhidrosis isn't just about overheating. It's about your brain, your muscles, your heart—everything needing a way to cool down, and your body just... refusing."*

I nodded. *"Yeah. I've pretty much lived my whole life planning my every move to avoid overheating."*

He leaned back in his chair. *"Do you know how we discovered anhidrosis?"*

I hesitated. *"I mean... I know it's rare. But I don't really know the history."*

He steepled his fingers. *"It started with horses."*

I blinked. *"Horses?"*

He nodded. *"Back in the early 1900s, trainers started noticing something strange. They would work their horses all day, exercising them in the heat, and then—out of nowhere—the horse would drop dead."*

I swallowed. *"What? Just like that?"*

"Just like that." He sighed. *"At first, they had no idea what was happening. The horses seemed strong, healthy—until they weren't. But when they studied the bodies afterward, they realized the issue."*

I sat forward. *"Which was?"*

"The horses weren't sweating."

A chill ran down my spine.

"Imagine running a marathon," Dr. Whitaker continued, *"but instead of sweating, your body just holds onto the heat. Your muscles overheat. Your brain—which is mostly protein—starts cooking, literally breaking down from the temperature. And then?"* He snapped his fingers. *"Your*

body shuts down."

I shuddered.

"That's why this isn't just a comfort issue," he said, voice firm. *"It's a medical necessity that you avoid overheating. And yet, people act like it's not a real disability simply because they can't see it."*

I nodded slowly. *"Tell me about it."*

Dr. Whitaker leaned forward. *"Which is why I'm prescribing you a handicapped parking permit."*

I blinked. *"Wait, what?"*

"You need it," he said simply. *"I've reviewed your history. I see how often you've suffered heat exhaustion, how many times you've nearly collapsed. You need close parking—not because it's convenient, but because crossing a hot parking lot could be dangerous for you."*

I had never even *considered* asking for one.

"I don't want to take a spot from someone who really needs it," I admitted.

Dr. Whitaker gave me a stern look. *"Lily. You do really need it. Just because you're not in a wheelchair doesn't mean your disability isn't real."*

His words sat heavy in my chest.

People didn't *see* my disability. And that's exactly why they didn't respect it.

––––––––––

Getting the handicapped parking tag should have been simple.

It wasn't.

When I went to the Department of Motor Vehicles, I handed my paperwork to the woman behind the counter. She barely glanced at it before scoffing.

"You don't look disabled," she said.

I tensed. *"I have a condition that prevents me from sweating. My doctor prescribed this so I can avoid overheating."*

She snorted. *"So, what? You just... get hot?"*

I clenched my fists. *"Yes. And if I overheat, I can pass out. It's a medical condition."*

She rolled her eyes, flipping through my paperwork lazily. *"We got people in wheelchairs who need these spots. You don't need it just 'cause you don't like the heat."*

The heat crawled up my neck—not from the temperature, but from frustration.

I wanted to yell, to demand she take me seriously. But I had been dismissed so many times before, I knew it wouldn't matter.

Instead, I forced myself to stay calm and said, *"I understand your skepticism, but my doctor approved this based on medical necessity. If you have a problem with it, you can call him directly."*

That shut her up.

With an irritated sigh, she stamped my papers and handed me the handicapped parking tag.

I took it and after I had collected my matching handicapped identification card, I walked out, jaw tight.

I had done everything right. I had medical proof, doctor's approval, and a legitimate disability—and yet, people still treated me like I was trying to cheat the system.

But nothing compared to the way strangers treated me in the parking lot.

I can't count the number of times an old white woman stopped me in a parking lot to demand I justify why I was parked in a handicapped space. It always started the same way. I would pull into the spot, hang my *DMV-issued tag*, step out of my car—and suddenly, I was on trial.

"Excuse me, young lady," they would call out, peering over their oversized sunglasses. *"That spot is for handicapped people."*

I would clench my jaw. "*I am handicapped.*"

They would scan me up and down, looking for a cane, a brace, something visible to satisfy their expectations.

Then came the classic: "*You don't look disabled.*"

And the one that always made my blood boil: "*You should be ashamed of yourself.*"

As if I had stolen something from them.

As if I hadn't spent my entire life *suffering* in ways they couldn't even begin to understand.

I tried explaining at first, tried reasoning with them. But eventually, I stopped wasting my breath.

They weren't asking because they cared.

They were asking because they believed disability had to be visible for it to be real.

But I knew better.

And if they had spent even one day in my body, they would too.

My disability wasn't one people could see. But that didn't mean it wasn't there. I had learned the hard way that some people would *never* believe me. That no amount of explaining, no amount of doctor's notes or medical facts, would ever make them understand.

And that's why, if you ever see someone parked in a handicapped space, and you're not sure if they "deserve" it?

Mind. Your. Own. Business.

Because the truth is—you have *no idea* what they're going through.

And your judgment?

It could be the most exhausting part of their disability.

———————

If there's one thing I've learned, it's that disability doesn't always look the way people expect it to.

When people think of disabilities, they think of wheelchairs, canes, hearing aids, prosthetic limbs—things they can *see*. They don't think about the conditions that exist quietly, invisibly, tucked beneath the surface of someone's everyday life.

They don't think about people like me.

And because of that, I've spent my life explaining myself to strangers who don't deserve an explanation.

But the truth is, I'm not alone in this. Not by a long shot.

When I was younger, I used to think I was one of the few people in the world dealing with something like this—

something that made everyday life feel like an obstacle course, something that set me apart in ways that weren't always visible.

But I was wrong.

According to the Centers for Disease Control and Prevention (CDC), 1 in 4 adults in the United States has some type of disability. That's 61 million people.

Let that sink in.

That means that when you walk down a crowded street, when you sit in a classroom, when you go to work—there's a good chance that someone around you is living with a disability. And you probably don't even realize it.

Some disabilities are obvious. But others? They exist in the quiet struggles people don't talk about.

Chronic pain that makes getting out of bed a daily battle.

Autoimmune disorders that drain every ounce of energy from a person's body.

Neurological conditions that make the simplest tasks feel impossible.

And then there are people like me—people whose bodies don't function the way they're supposed to in ways that aren't immediately apparent to the outside world. That's the thing about disabilities. They don't come with a neon sign that says, *"This is why I'm struggling."*

But that doesn't make them any less real.

When someone has a visible disability, people don't question it. They don't demand proof, don't roll their eyes, don't whisper about whether or not they're "faking."

But when your disability is invisible? People become the worst versions of themselves. I can't tell you how many times I've heard:

"You don't look disabled."—cringe!

"You're too young to have a real health issue."

"You're just being dramatic."

And my personal favorite—*"It can't be that bad."*

But here's the thing: If you can't see someone's disability, it's because you haven't been paying attention. Because most times, if you really looked, you'd see the exhaustion in their eyes. The careful way they move. The way they subtly adjust their day to accommodate something they didn't ask for.

It's not always a cane or a wheelchair.

Sometimes, it's someone like me parking in a handicapped spot because they know walking across a sweltering parking lot could send their body into shutdown mode.

Sometimes, it's someone choosing a booth in a restaurant instead of a chair because sitting for too long causes unbearable pain.

Sometimes, it's someone declining an invitation because they don't have the energy to explain, yet again, why they can't *"just push through."*

We don't owe the world an explanation.

But we spend so much time giving one anyway—because the world has convinced itself that if you can't *see* something, it must not be real. Tuh...Amen?

So, here's what I wish more people understood:

Disability is part of human existence.

It's not something rare or unusual. It's not a "tragedy" that happens to a select few. It's just *a part of life*—one that millions of people navigate every single day.

And if you don't have a disability now, that doesn't mean you never will. Aging. Illness. Injury. Genetics. These things don't ask for permission. They don't care how much money you have, how fit you are, how much you think it could never happen to you.

That's why empathy matters.

Because at some point in life, you or someone you love will experience a body or mind that doesn't work the way it's supposed to.

And when that day comes, you'll want understanding.

You'll want patience.

You'll want people to *believe you* when you say you're struggling.

So, if you're lucky enough to be *able-bodied* today, use that privilege for something good. Don't make someone explain why they need accommodations. Don't assume someone is lying just because their disability isn't obvious. Don't scoff at the person using a handicapped space just because they don't have a cane or a wheelchair.

Instead?

Just be kind.

Because at the end of the day, no one should have to *prove* they deserve respect.

And if you're ever in doubt?

Mind your own business.

CHAPTER SEVEN

COLLEGE & CAREER

I didn't start sweating "all the time" after that day in the car. My body still had its struggles. I still had to be careful. But I no longer felt completely at war with myself.

I knew, deep down, that my body was trying.

It just needed help figuring out how.

That didn't mean my life suddenly became easy.

Despite this newfound glimpse of hope, my body still operated on its own unpredictable rules. I could go weeks without a single drop of sweat and then, out of nowhere, feel damp after sitting in a hot car. I could be in a humid room and feel like I was suffocating, or I could be outside on a hot day and feel... fine. There was no consistency, no pattern to rely on. I still had to watch the signs, still had to know when to stop before my body made the decision for me.

And as much as I wanted to believe that I had turned a corner, there were still moments that reminded me—I would never function like everyone else.

Washington, D.C. was one of those moments.

The trip had been Marcus's idea.

"We should do something fun before summer classes start," he had said one evening over the phone. *"You ever been to D.C.?"*

"No," I admitted, sitting on my bed with my legs crossed. *"Maya has, though. She went for a class trip a few years ago."*

*"Then we **have** to go,"* he said, like it was already settled. *"Be tourists for a day. See the monuments, eat overpriced street food, the whole thing."*

I hesitated. A trip like that meant *a lot* of walking. And while I had been getting better at handling my heat sensitivity, I wasn't exactly built for *hours of sightseeing under the sun.*

But before I could overthink it, Maya—who had been listening in on speakerphone—gasped dramatically. *"Oh my God, YES. You have to go!"*

I laughed. *"Why are you more excited than me?"*

"Because this is a huge deal, Lil!" she said. *"Your first official 'couples trip'. The nation's capital! With your 'boyfriend'. Walking hand-in-hand past historic landmarks like y'all are in some kind of romantic movie montage."*

Marcus chuckled. *"Maya, you should be a travel agent."*

"I should," she agreed, then turned her attention back to me. *"But seriously, you need to do this. You deserve to have fun. And if you start overheating, just—sit in a museum or something. Boom, problem solved."*

She made it sound so simple.

And maybe… maybe it could be.

Because if there was one thing I had learned since that night at prom, it was that Marcus had a way of making me feel *safe*—in a way I never had before.

It wasn't just about the way he looked at me, or the way he always listened when I talked. It was the way he reacted when I needed him most. The way he instinctively *knew* when to step in, when to offer help without making me feel like I was helpless.

The first time I nearly overheated in front of him, he didn't panic.

He didn't look at me like I was fragile.

He just *acted*.

We had been at an outdoor event with some of his friends, and after too much sun, too much standing, too much *everything*, I felt my body slipping into that dangerous zone of overheating.

I had barely managed to whisper, "*Marcus, I need to sit,*" before he was already guiding me toward the shade, kneeling next to me like it was just another part of the day. He pulled a bottle of water from his bag—because of course he carried one, just in case I ever needed it—and told his friends, "*Go ahead, we'll catch up later.*"

No questions. No making a scene.

Just *trust*.

And he had never broken it.

That's why, when he asked if I wanted to take a trip to D.C., I didn't immediately shut it down.

I knew my body had a mind of its own.

I knew *walking for hours in the sun* could be dangerous for me.

But I also knew that if something happened—if I needed to stop, if I needed to rest—Marcus would be there. No judgment. No hesitation. Just him, making sure I was okay.

And if I was going to experience something like this, there was no one else—besides Maya—that I would want to do it with.

"*Alright,*" I said, smiling. "*Let's do it.*"

The weather was perfect. A crisp, mild spring day with just enough warmth to make it comfortable but not suffocating. It wasn't even 70 degrees. *Seventy!* The kind of day where normal people could walk for hours without breaking a sweat.

I should have been fine.

And at first, I was.

Marcus and I started at the Washington Monument, craning our necks to take in the towering obelisk against the clear blue sky.

"*Did you know,*" Marcus said, slipping effortlessly into his 'fun-fact mode', "*that the Washington Monument was supposed to have a capstone made out of solid gold?*"

I snorted. "*Why does that sound like something rich people would do?*"

"*Right? But they went with aluminum instead because it was considered 'even rarer' than gold back then.*"

I arched an eyebrow. "*I'm gonna fact-check that later.*"

"*Please do,*" he grinned, taking my hand.

From there, we made our way toward the Lincoln Memorial, stopping along the Reflecting Pool to take pictures. We did the cheesy tourist poses—Marcus pretending to "hold" the Washington Monument between his fingers, me pointing dramatically at the distance like I was giving a historic speech.

It was *fun*.

It was the kind of fun I had spent *years* watching other people have, the kind of fun I had convinced myself I would never get to experience.

We stopped at a street vendor and grabbed ice cream cones, standing near the iconic columns as we let the cold sweetness melt against our tongues.

Marcus bumped his shoulder into mine. *"This is nice."*

I smiled. *"Yeah. It really is."*

I felt *normal*.

For a little while.

The thing about my condition is that it doesn't care about the weather.

It doesn't care if the temperature is technically mild. It doesn't care if other people are comfortable. It only cares about one thing: whether my body can keep up.

And after hours of walking, my body *couldn't*.

We had just finished taking pictures at the World War II Memorial when I felt it—the slow, creeping signs of overheating.

My head started buzzing, like the world was getting too loud.

My chest felt heavier.

My skin wasn't burning yet, but I knew what was coming. The dizziness. The nausea. The feeling that I was seconds away from shutting down completely.

I had to stop. *Now.*

Without thinking, I muttered, *"Marcus, I need to sit,"* and then—

I *laid down*. Right there. On the sidewalk.

Flat on my back, eyes squeezed shut, arms spread out like I was making a snow angel on the concrete.

I *knew* people were staring. I *knew* I looked ridiculous. But I also knew that if I didn't *go down voluntarily*, I was going to *face-plant involuntarily.*

Marcus was immediately next to me, blocking me from view as best as he could. *"Hey, hey. You okay?"*

I nodded weakly. *"Just need a second."*

He didn't ask questions. He didn't panic. He just sat next to me, cross-legged on the sidewalk, like it was the most normal thing in the world.

If people whispered, he ignored them. If they stared, he didn't care.

After a few minutes, when the dizziness started to fade, I let out a slow breath. *"Well. That was embarrassing."*

Marcus grinned. *"Eh. You pulled it off. Real casual."*

I rolled my eyes. *"Uh-huh. Totally casual to collapse in front of the Lincoln Memorial."*

"Hey," he said, his voice suddenly serious. *"You don't have to be embarrassed. You know that, right? And this is the World War II Memorial."*

I swallowed. *"I know. It's just—"*

I sighed. *"People always say, 'Oh, not sweating isn't a big deal.' But if it's not a big deal, then why does everybody else do it? I always say this! People just do not get it!"*

Marcus nodded. *"Exactly."*

"This right here?" I gestured to the sidewalk beneath me. *"This is proof that it matters. It's not just an inconvenience. It's my body shutting down because it doesn't know how to keep up."*

Marcus reached for my hand. *"And that's why I'm here— to remind you that you don't have to keep up with anyone but yourself."*

I squeezed his hand back.

He helped me up, and we found a shady spot to rest. We took the rest of the day *slow*, adjusting the plans to work for *me*.

And that was the difference.

I didn't feel like a burden.

I felt understood.

That made all the difference.

———————

Summer classes flew by in a blur of coursework, late-night study sessions, and long phone calls with Marcus. We didn't get to see each other as much as we wanted, but when we did, it felt effortless. He had become a fixture in my life—steady, unwavering, present.

And after how well our trip to D.C. had gone, we decided to take another.

This time? *The beach.*

I had my hesitations. The idea of being under the direct sun for hours made me nervous, but Marcus was prepared.

"We'll bring a tent," he said, showing me his list of supplies like he was planning a military operation. *"Extra*

cold water, cooling towels, and we'll take breaks in the shade whenever you need."

He made it so easy to say yes.

And surprisingly? I was *fine.*

The breeze from the ocean kept me cool, and unlike walking around D.C., I wasn't constantly moving. When I got too warm, I waded into the waves, letting the water regulate my body the way it always had.

I didn't feel like I had to fight to enjoy myself.

Marcus held my hand as we walked along the shore, the setting sun painting the sky in hues of orange and pink. *"You're doing it again,"* he said softly. *"Living."*

I squeezed his fingers. *"Yeah. I think I am."*

It was the perfect end to the summer.

But life was always moving, and before I knew it, fall semester had begun.

If summer had been *freedom*, fall was *a whirlwind.*

Classes were heavier, coursework more demanding, and suddenly, my perfectly balanced life felt a little off-kilter.

And Maya?

I was seeing her less.

Not because anything was wrong—she was still Maya, still my best friend—but we were both busier than ever.

We had different class schedules, different obligations pulling us in opposite directions. She had taken on an extra research project, and between that, her coursework, and my job, our usual meetups became less frequent.

We still texted. Still sent each other memes in the middle of the night. Still called when we could.

But something about it felt... different.

Not in a bad way, exactly. Just different.

For the first time, it hit me that growing up meant shifting tides—not everything could stay the same.

Maya had her own path.

And I had mine.

That's what made my job at the call center so important. It wasn't just a paycheck. It wasn't just something to do between classes.

It was stability.

It was purpose.

It was the thing that kept me grounded as life kept changing around me.

I wasn't alone.

I was part of something bigger.

Sitting at my desk, headset on, fingers poised over the keyboard, I listened to at least one hundred calls per shift. Helping people made everything worth it—even on days when my own body felt like an obstacle.

And today, with the rain pouring outside, something told me it was going to be an important one.

I had spent most of my life feeling like I was battling my own body. Learning how to regulate my temperature when my body refused to do it for me wasn't just exhausting—it was isolating.

But over the years, I had learned how to cope.

I had learned to find my own balance, to anticipate the signs, to control what I could and accept what I couldn't. I had built a system around myself—choosing classes that kept me indoors during the hottest parts of the day, keeping an emergency cooling towel in my backpack, and never leaving home without extra water.

And through it all, I had found solace in rainy days.

When the rain came, I could breathe easier. The air felt cleaner, softer against my skin. People always complained about rainy days, grumbling about wet clothes and muddy sidewalks, but to me, rain was freedom.

And, in a way, so was this job.

I worked part-time at the hospital's triage call center, and I loved it.

People didn't call 911 if they weren't sure their situation was an emergency. Instead, they called us—the intake workers—who helped them decide whether they needed immediate medical attention or could be connected with a nurse for guidance.

I sat in a small but busy office, in a slightly uncomfortable chair, typing as quickly as I could while patients described their symptoms over the phone.

"Okay, ma'am, I understand. I'm entering that information now," I'd say, keeping my voice calm even when the person on the other end was frantic. *"The system will triage your symptoms and provide a condition in just a moment. Can you confirm your full name and date of birth?"*

The computer program would then assess their symptoms and direct me to refer them to the appropriate nurse or advise them to head to the emergency room immediately.

I wasn't a doctor. I wasn't even a nurse.

But I was helping people, and that meant everything to me.

That evening, the rain was relentless.

The parking lot was practically flooding, and the hospital lobby was filled with soaked visitors shaking out their umbrellas. The sound of raindrops hammering against the windows was soothing, and as I worked through my calls, I felt calmer than usual—the weight of the day lifted by the rhythmic tap of the storm outside.

I wasn't the only one who felt it.

"*Lily,*" Nurse Janice, my favorite nurse on shift, leaned over from her desk, smiling. "*This weather is just perfect isn't it?*"

I grinned. "*Finally! Someone who gets it.*"

Most people in the office complained about the rain, but not Janice. She was one of the few who loved it as much as I did.

Nurse Janice was an older woman, maybe in her late fifties, with warm brown skin, deep laugh lines around her mouth, and a voice that could calm even the most panicked caller. She had been working in the medical field for decades, and I had never once seen her flustered.

"*You know,*" she continued, glancing out at the storm, "*when I was your age, I used to sit by the window just to feel the cool breeze after the rain.*"

I leaned back in my chair. "*Same here. It's the only time I feel normal, like my body is finally in sync with the world.*"

Janice gave me a knowing smile. "*I can understand that.*"

She always had a way of making me feel seen, even when we weren't talking about anything deep.

And today, I was feeling brave enough to talk about something that had been on my mind for years. I never wanted to consider the morbid possibility so I always decided against broaching the subject with anyone. But Nurse Janice was *a nurse!* If anyone had any advice, it would be her.

I had just finished up my fourth "pregnancy concern" intake of the night. Each one was for a different concern and I had to refer two of them to the ER. Once the calls had tapered down, I hesitated for a moment before speaking.

"*Janice,*" I said, lowering my voice. "*I've been thinking a lot about something, and I don't know if I'm just overthinking it.*"

She turned her attention to me fully. "*What's on your mind, sweetheart?*"

I swallowed. "*It's just… growing up, I always worried about how my body doesn't sweat, right?*"

She nodded, listening carefully.

"*Well,*" I continued, "*now that I'm older, I've started thinking about the future. And honestly? I'm terrified of pregnancy.*"

Her brows lifted slightly, but she didn't interrupt.

"I've seen movies, TV shows... Every woman in labor is covered in sweat. I mean, completely drenched. And I keep thinking—what if I can't handle it? What if my body literally can't cool itself down during something that intense?"

Janice's expression softened, and she reached over, squeezing my hand. *"That's a real fear, Lily. I understand why you'd be worried."*

I let out a nervous laugh. *"It's just... nobody ever talks about how pregnancy affects people with conditions like mine. There's nothing out there to tell me if it's safe, if I'll be okay. And it's not like I can just test it out ahead of time, you know?"*

Janice's eyes twinkled with something I couldn't quite place. Then she said something that changed everything.

"Lily," she said, her voice gentle, *"you don't have to worry about that anymore."*

I frowned. *"What do you mean?"*

She let out a small chuckle. *"Because I've never sweat a day in my life either. And I've had two kids."*

I blinked.

For a moment, I thought I had misheard her.

"You—what?"

Janice smiled. *"That's right. I don't sweat, either. Never have. Not as a child, not as an adult, and not even when I was giving birth."*

I stared at her.

"You—wait—you've never—ever?"

She shook her head. *"Nope. And let me tell you something, Lily—both my babies were born just fine."*

I felt my entire world tilt.

"But... how?"

Janice chuckled again. *"The human body is an amazing thing. It finds ways to adapt. I made sure to stay hydrated, had cool towels on me, and kept the labor room as cold as they'd let me. And you know what? I did just fine."*

I felt my chest tighten—not with anxiety, but with something else entirely.

Relief.

For *years* this fear had loomed over me, whispering that I was different, that I wasn't built to do what so many women could do effortlessly.

But sitting here, in this little call center, on this rainy evening I had just heard the one thing I never thought I'd hear—proof that someone like me had already done it.

And that meant…

So could I.

I sat there, letting the truth of Janice's words settle into my bones.

For so long, I had accepted that there were things in life I would never be able to do. I had trained myself to expect limitations. To assume that my body would always hold me back.

But here was Janice—living proof that my fears weren't as absolute as I thought.

She smiled at me knowingly. *"I don't know what the future holds for you, Lily. But if this is something you want one day, don't be afraid of it. You're stronger than you think."*

I nodded, swallowing hard. *"Thank you, Janice. Really."*

She squeezed my hand once more before letting go. *"Now, get back to work before they dock our pay,"* she teased.

I laughed, shaking my head.

As I turned back to my screen, listening to the rain pour outside, I felt something I hadn't in a long time.

Reassurance.

I didn't have all the answers.

I still had challenges ahead.

But for the first time, I wasn't afraid of my own future. I was excited and ready to embrace it.

———————

CHAPTER EIGHT

MOTHERHOOD &
TRANSFORMATION

The rain had always been my safe place.

Ever since that conversation with Nurse Janice on that fateful rainy day, something inside me had shifted. Maybe it was the simple acknowledgment that my body, while unpredictable, was not completely incapable. Maybe it was realizing that I had more control over my well-being than I had ever allowed myself to believe. Whatever it was, it had led me here—this version of myself that I never thought possible.

I had become *intentional.*

I took care of myself in ways I never had before. Drinking more water. Prioritizing rest. Managing stress. Choosing foods that fueled me instead of drained me.

I started moving more—not because I had to, but because I wanted to know what my body was capable of.

At first, it was stretching—something simple. Just a few minutes in the morning, rolling my shoulders, reaching my arms high above my head. Then, I started following along with short yoga routines I found online. Nothing strenuous, just movements that helped me feel more connected to myself and prepare my body for the day.

Then came walking.

Not just from one air-conditioned space to another—but intentional walks. Long careful strolls in the early evening, when the sun hung lower in the sky, the air cooling just enough for me to breathe comfortably. Sometimes I'd have Maya or Marcus by my side, sometimes I'd be alone, letting the world melt away with every step.

I even did some strength training—because, why not? If my body needed help learning how to regulate itself, I'd give it the best shot I could.

It wasn't about achieving perfection. It was about working *with* my body instead of fighting it every step of the way.

And I realized something.

The heat didn't own me.

I had spent years fearing it, avoiding it, letting it dictate my life. But now?

Now, I was learning how to navigate it.

I still had limits. I still had to be careful. But now, I was stepping beyond survival and into discovery.

The real change—the life-altering shift—wasn't just in my habits. It was in my mindset.

Before I met Nurse Janice, my life had always been dictated by limitations. I measured everything by what I *couldn't* do, what I *had* to avoid, what would be *too risky*. My condition had drawn invisible lines around my existence, and for as long as I could remember, I stayed within them.

But something about that conversation with her—about how I was stronger than I gave myself credit for, about how my body wasn't broken but just needed different things— had planted a seed in my mind.

A question I had never dared to ask myself before.

What if I can?

It started small, almost imperceptibly at first.

I would catch myself about to say, *I can't do that,* but then stop. Not because I had suddenly decided to be reckless, but because I realized—I had never really *tried* that thing. I had spent my life making pre-conceived assumptions about my limits rather than exploring them.

So, I started experimenting.

Could I go for a walk in the early evening instead of assuming the heat would overwhelm me?

Could I take a road trip somewhere without the constant fear of overheating?

Could I challenge myself—not to prove something to others, but to see just how much I had been holding myself back?

And time and time again, I found that my body was willing to work with me, if I gave it a fair chance.

For so long, I had seen my body as something that worked *against* me. But what if—just maybe—it was trying to work *with* me?

Maybe it wasn't about pushing through pain. Maybe it was about understanding it.

Maybe it wasn't about forcing my body to act like everyone else's. Maybe it was about learning its language, listening to what it needed, adapting in ways I had never considered before.

That's what Janice had given me—the realization that I had choices. That I could experiment without fear of failure. That I could take small steps toward the life I wanted, instead of standing still in the one I thought I was stuck with.

And through every high and low, Maya and Marcus were right there beside me.

Maya cheered me on when I told her I had gone for a walk without immediately feeling exhausted. She was always hyping me up and reminding me how far I had come.

Marcus was my steady anchor, making sure I never felt like I had to do it all alone. He held my hand when I nervously stepped onto a hiking trail for the first time, my heart pounding as I took in the long stretch of dirt path ahead.

"You don't have to prove anything," he had said, squeezing my fingers gently.

"I know," I had whispered. *"I just... want to see if I can."*

And I took that first step.

It took years, but I graduated from college feeling stronger, healthier, and more at peace with my body than I had ever been.

And somewhere in between all of that personal growth, I had fallen even deeper in love with Marcus. No matter how things changed, my relationship with him felt like something straight out of a well-written Lifetime movie—effortless, natural, like every moment was falling into place exactly as it was meant to.

Marcus had a way of making me feel seen, always treating me with a grace that felt both comforting and empowering. His love wasn't just something he said—it was in every action, every gesture.

I remember our first year of dating—how every small milestone felt monumental, how being with him felt like slipping into a space that had been waiting for me all along.

It wasn't some grand, movie-worthy moment. There were no fireworks, no dramatic declarations under a starry sky.

It was in the small things.

It was in the way he always saved me a seat, no matter where we were—whether in the library during finals week or at Maya's crowded apartment when we all crammed in to watch movies.

It was in the way he learned my routines and adapted to them, carrying an extra bottle of water for me in his backpack, just in case. The way he would instinctively walk on the shadier side of the street so I wouldn't overheat. The way he could tell when I needed a break before I even had to say it.

It was in the way he made me feel like I wasn't different.

Like I was just *Lily*.

And then there were the big moments—the ones where our worlds truly started to merge.

The first time Marcus brought me to meet his family, I was terrified.

Not because I thought they wouldn't like me—but because meeting someone's family was *serious*. It meant we weren't just some casual campus couple sneaking kisses between classes. It meant we were *real.*

And Marcus came from a big family.

"Just a heads-up," he told me as we pulled into the driveway of his parents' house, *"my mom is going to try to feed you immediately, my dad will probably ask you about your career goals within the first five minutes, and my cousin Devin—"* he groaned, shaking his head—*"is going to act like he's the funniest person alive. Just... ignore him."*

I laughed, squeezing his hand. *"Sounds like a good time."*

I *thought* I was ready.

I wasn't.

The moment I stepped inside, I was hit with the overwhelming smell of spices, grilled meats, and something sweet baking in the oven. A group of relatives were packed into the kitchen, laughing loudly over some inside joke. Kids zoomed through the hallway at full speed, nearly knocking into me as they yelled something about a rematch in *Mario Kart.*

Marcus's mom spotted us first.

"There's my baby!" she called out, practically beaming as she pulled Marcus into a tight hug. Then she turned to me, her eyes softening. *"And you must be Lily."*

I nodded, offering a shy smile. *"Yes, ma'am."*

She took one look at me, then grabbed my face in both hands like she had known me forever. *"Oh, honey. You are beautiful."*

I barely had time to respond before she was dragging me into the kitchen, already piling a plate full of food.

Marcus had warned me, but I hadn't been prepared.

Everywhere I turned, someone was introducing themselves, asking me questions, or telling me some embarrassing story about Marcus as a kid. His dad grilled me on my future plans within *four minutes*, his sister asked how long we had been dating with a knowing smirk, and—just as promised—his cousin Devin was doing way too much.

"So, Lily," Devin said, plopping down next to me at the dinner table. *"What's your favorite conspiracy theory?"*

I blinked. *"I... uh, I don't really—"*

He waved a hand. *"Okay, okay. Fine. What about time travel? You think it's real?"*

I opened my mouth, then shut it again. *"I—"*

Marcus groaned from across the table. *"Devin, please."*

I couldn't help but laugh.

His family was *chaotic*.

And I loved every second of it.

After that first introduction, it didn't take long for me to become a regular fixture at Marcus's family gatherings.

By the time Fourth of July rolled around, I was expected to be there.

"*You **better** show up,*" his mom had texted me the week before. "*I need backup on the potato salad situation.*"

I had no idea what that meant, but I wasn't about to question it.

The cookout was massive—relatives, friends, random neighbors who somehow always ended up with a plate. Kids ran around with sparklers, someone's uncle had parked himself at the grill with an oversized apron that read *The Grillfather*, and there was an ongoing debate about who made the best ribs.

And, of course, there was Devin.

"*Alright, Lily,*" he said, sidling up next to me as I fixed a plate. "*Time for the real test.*"

I raised an eyebrow. "*Which is?*"

He gestured toward the spades table.

I let out a nervous laugh. "*Oh, no. I don't play spades.*"

The table went silent.

All conversation stopped.

Even the kids seemed to freeze in place.

Marcus, standing behind me, closed his eyes like he was in physical pain.

His aunt, who had been mid-sip of her lemonade, set her cup down very slowly.

"You don't... play?" she asked, voice carefully neutral.

I glanced at Marcus for help. He shook his head. *"I can't save you."*

Devin sighed, shaking his head like I had personally disappointed him.

"Alright," he said. *"We'll fix that. Come sit down."*

And that's how I got dragged into a spades lesson in the middle of a Fourth of July cookout.

Marcus sat behind me, watching in pure amusement as Devin and his aunt walked me through the basics.

"You do not renege," his aunt warned. *"That's how fights start."*

I nodded solemnly. *"Understood."*

By the end of the night, I wasn't good, but at least I wasn't a disgrace.

And, more importantly—I felt *at home*.

That's the thing about falling in love. It's not just about the big romantic gestures. It's about family cookouts, about laughing until your stomach hurts, about sitting next to someone's grandma while she tells you a story she's already told five times before.

It's about road trips with no destination, about knowing how the other person likes their coffee, about texting them when you see something that reminds you of them.

It's Marcus standing next to me on a random Tuesday, making pasta in my tiny college apartment, swaying to music only he can hear.

It's the way his hand automatically finds mine in a crowded room.

It's the way I feel when I'm with him—like I am exactly where I am meant to be.

And in those moments, I know—

This love?

This is forever.

We got engaged on a drizzly spring evening, the two of us standing under a canopy of oak trees, the air thick with the scent of fresh rain. The moment he pulled the ring out of his pocket, I could feel every version of myself—the girl who once sat on the sidelines, the teenager who fought against a body that didn't work the way she wanted, the young woman learning to trust herself—collide into one.

I said yes before he could even finish asking.

And just as I threw my arms around him, I heard a muffled squeal from somewhere in the trees.

Marcus groaned, laughing under his breath. *"Maya, I know you're back there."*

A moment later, Maya burst out from behind a thick oak, phone in hand, beaming like she had just won the lottery. *"Oh, don't mind me! Just capturing history!"*

I gasped, eyes wide. *"You **knew**?"*

Marcus smirked. *"Of course I knew. I needed backup to make sure everything was perfect."*

Maya jogged toward us, waving the phone like a prized trophy. *"I got the whole thing on video. And, Lily, you were so cute! The way you said yes before he even finished? Iconic."*

I covered my face, laughing. *"Oh my God."*

She grabbed my hands, squeezing tight. *"I am so proud of you. Of both of you."* Then she turned to Marcus, pointing a playful finger at him. *"And you? You're officially stuck with us forever now. Hope you're ready."*

Marcus chuckled. *"Wouldn't have it any other way."*

I looked between the two of them—my best friend, my soon-to-be husband, the two people who had held me up through every phase of my life—and felt my heart swell.

This wasn't just an engagement. This was the moment I realized *I had always been surrounded by love.*

We got married a year later.

And life, in all its unpredictability, led us down paths we never could have imagined.

Marcus flourished in his career, and I found purpose in unexpected places.

I took on a role at a non-profit, working part-time to support underserved communities. I began teaching English as a Second Language to adults who had spent their lives unable to read or write. Watching their confidence grow with each new word they learned reminded me so much of my own journey—it wasn't about how long it took; it was about finally finding a way forward.

I also ran a community garden, a project close to my heart, where families could come together, grow their own food, and learn the joy of nurturing something from the ground up.

And after school, I worked with kids, giving them a space where they could learn, explore, and be seen.

Life wasn't perfect, but it was full.

And then, one day, Marcus and I started to talk about expanding our little world.

The decision to become parents wasn't a sudden realization. It was a slow, steady conversation that stretched over months, woven between quiet mornings over coffee and late-night talks under the covers.

"Do you think we're ready?" I asked one evening, lying on the couch with my legs draped over Marcus's lap.

He tilted his head, considering my question. *"Do you think anyone is ever really **ready**?"*

I exhaled a soft laugh. *"Probably not."*

But the thought had already taken root in my mind.

I had spent my whole life navigating what my body could and couldn't do. But now? Now, I wanted to see what it was capable of in a new way.

Could I carry a child? Would my condition make it difficult? Would pregnancy make me more vulnerable to overheating? The questions spun in my head, but this time, I wasn't afraid of them.

Because I knew, no matter what happened, I wasn't alone.

Marcus squeezed my hand. *"If this is something we want, we'll figure it out. Just like we always do."*

I smiled. *"Then let's try."*

And with that, we stepped into a new chapter of our lives—one that would change me in ways I never saw coming.

From the moment I saw the two pink lines on the test, a mix of emotions flooded me—excitement, nervousness, awe.

I had spent my whole life feeling incapable, like my body hated me. But now? Now, it was creating life.

The months that followed were a whirlwind of firsts.

First heartbeat.

First kick.

First moment where I realized that for the first time in my life, my body wasn't just surviving—it was thriving.

Something about pregnancy changed me in ways I never could have predicted. I became more heat tolerant. My body, which had spent decades struggling to regulate its temperature, suddenly seemed to *understand* what to do.

It wasn't perfect. There were still challenges. Still moments where I had to be careful.

But I was stronger than I had ever been.

And when the day finally came, when I held our daughter in my arms for the first time, I knew—this was the moment everything had led me to.

———————

CHAPTER NINE

A NEW APPRECIATION

S he was tiny, fragile, *perfect*.

Her skin was impossibly soft, her fingers barely longer than my knuckles. The weight of her against my chest felt like something I had been waiting for my entire life without ever realizing it.

Marcus sat beside me in the hospital bed, one arm wrapped around my shoulders, the other gently tracing a fingertip over our daughter's impossibly small hand. She twitched in her sleep at the sensation, her little fingers curling instinctively around his.

"She's really here," I whispered.

"She is," he murmured. *"And she's ours."*

We had talked for months about what to name her, tossing around ideas, making lists, crossing them out. But in the end, there was only one name that felt right.

***Rain*.**

The element that had once been my refuge. The thing that had given me relief when my own body wouldn't. The one thing Marcus and I had always shared a love for.

And now, our daughter would carry it with her forever.

I kissed the top of her head, inhaling the faint scent of newborn skin. "*Rain,*" I whispered. "*Welcome to the world, baby girl.*"

Marcus grinned, pressing a kiss against my temple. "*Rain,*" he echoed, the name settling between us like something sacred.

And just like that, our world became hers.

Nothing prepares you for the beautiful chaos of new parenthood.

There were books, of course. Advice from doctors. Wisdom from friends and family. But none of it could truly capture the reality of what it meant to bring a tiny, helpless human into the world and suddenly be responsible for keeping them alive.

The first few nights were a blur of sleepless hours, of bleary-eyed feedings, of me and Marcus stumbling through the house in the dark, whispering, *Whose turn is it?* while trying to soothe a newborn who had no interest in the concept of night and day.

Breastfeeding was a challenge I hadn't fully anticipated.

I had assumed it would come naturally, but the reality was far from effortless. The latching struggles, the endless feedings, the exhaustion that settled into my bones like a second skin—it was overwhelming. I had read about the hormone shifts, about the way new mothers could find themselves in tears for no reason at all, but experiencing it firsthand was something else entirely.

There were moments when I felt *inadequate,* like I was failing her.

But then there were moments—quiet, sacred moments—when Rain would nestle against me, her tiny body trusting mine completely, and I would feel something powerful settle inside me.

She didn't need me to be perfect. She just needed me to be there.

Marcus, as always, was my rock.

He changed diapers half-asleep at 3 a.m. without complaint. He became an expert at swaddling, wrapping Rain up so snugly that she looked like a tiny burrito. He held her against his chest for hours, humming softly, walking up and down the hallways when she refused to sleep.

We were tired.

We were delirious.

We were in awe.

———————

The first time it rained after we brought Rain home, I stood at the window with her in my arms, watching the droplets slide down the glass.

She was only a few weeks old, her head still wobbly, her eyes wide and curious as she took in the world around her.

I smiled down at her. *"You hear that?"* I whispered. *"That's your name."*

Marcus came up behind me, wrapping his arms around us both. *"She's going to love the rain, just like her parents."*

I leaned into him, closing my eyes. For the first time in my life, I didn't fear the heat. I didn't long for relief.

I had already found it.

Not just in the rain.

But in this life we had built.

Raising a child is equal parts joy and exhaustion.

Yes, there were sleepless nights, early morning feedings, days when I barely had time to shower, and moments when I wondered if I was doing anything right.

But there was also laughter. Soft baby giggles. Tiny hands gripping mine. First words, first steps, first everything.

Every single day, my body continued to surprise me.

I chased after my daughter in the park without feeling like I would collapse from the heat.

I took her to the beach and let the sun warm my skin without immediately seeking shade.

I carried her in my arms, knowing that my body was capable.

Maya was there, for every milestone—the best aunt in the world. She spoiled my daughter in the best way possible, showering her with love, books, and endless stories about how her mother had once been just a nerdy girl who hated the heat.

Marcus, as always, was perfect. He was the kind of father I always knew he would be—patient, kind, completely smitten with our little girl.

And me?

I was still Lily. Still learning, still growing, still navigating this beautifully complicated body of mine.

But I no longer felt like I was fighting against it.

I had learned to rely on it. To love it.

And in doing so, I had found something I never thought possible—*peace*.

––––––––––

Months passed, and I slowly grew into motherhood the way one grows into a familiar sweater—tentative at first, then comfortably, like it had always been a part of me. I learned to trust myself. To trust my instincts. To let go of the fear that had once ruled me.

And one afternoon, as the clouds rolled in, the air thick with the promise of rain, I knew exactly what we needed to do.

"Marcus," I called, scooping Rain into my arms. *"Come outside with us."*

He raised an eyebrow but didn't question it, following me onto the back porch just as the first drops of rain began to fall.

I stepped barefoot onto the grass, letting the cool droplets land against my skin. Rain blinked up at the sky, her tiny fingers curling, her eyes filled with pure wonder.

For years, the rain had been my sanctuary.

And now?

Now, it was a celebration.

I spun slowly, laughing as Marcus joined us, his arms wrapping around me, his forehead pressed against mine.

"*I love you,*" I whispered.

He kissed me softly. "*I love you too.*"

And in that moment, I realized—

I had spent my life struggling with things I couldn't control.

But now?

Now, I had learned to embrace them.

And I had never felt freer.

---

www.ingramcontent.com/pod-product-compliance
Lightning Source LLC
Chambersburg PA
CBHW020659260626
47157CB00008B/3091